"Got a light, bud?" the dark man asked.

Johnny stopped, reached impatiently for his lighter. As he flicked it into flame the man's right hand shot up and caught him solidly under the ear. He rocked sideways into an iron fence and bounced off into a hard left to the body.

"Maybe you'll mind your own business after this, bud!" the man rasped. He launched another right hand.

Johnny blocked the punch, caught the hand and dragged the body behind it in close. He threw his massive weight into a low gut punch and caught the man as he sagged. He lifted the limp body, carried it over to the fence, and hung it by its coat collar from an iron pike.

"Now start talkin' and save yourself wear-and-tear," he growled.

That's Johnny Killain, six-feet-plus of high explosive triggered for violence. He prowls the night world of a big-city hotel, and the people he meets are not always gentle. Especially when he's on the trail of a killer . . .

KILLER WITH A

DAN MARLOWE

KEY

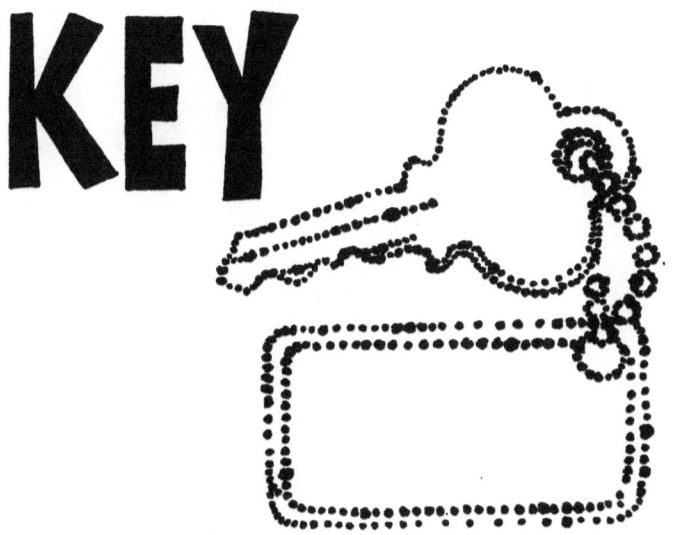

WILDSIDE PRESS

JOHNNY KILLAIN COULD SEE Jeff Landry's slender figure shiningly reflected from the bronzed walls of the service elevator, diminutive alongside his own bulk in its blue-gray uniform. He threw open the cab door and glanced out over the lobby before turning to look inquiringly at the blond man and nodding in the direction of the bar. "One for the road, Jeff? You might like Tommy's better."

Jeff Landry shook his head apologetically. "I know I've been poor company, Johnny, but it wasn't your drinks."

"So why rush off? You just got here. I don't see you all that often."

"Restless, I guess."

"Just what is it that's botherin' you, Jeff? An' in case you've forgotten I already asked you the same thing upstairs. You act like a man with something on his mind."

"It'll keep," the slender man said lightly. "When am I going to see you over at my place? We put the animals to bed any time after eight, you know."

"I'll get over there, for sure. I know I keep sayin' that, but I will. Business bad, Jeff?"

Jeff Landry's lips tightened. "Business is . . . well, actually, business is fine, Johnny."

"That's not what you started to say, though."

"No third degree, now." The blond man smiled. He turned left, toward the foyer. "Don't mind my bad manners—please? And thanks for the drinks."

"I'll be over to lower the level on your bottle."

"You do that." Jeff Landry waved as he exited, and Johnny looked after him thoughtfully. He had known Jeff Landry for some time, and this abrupt departure after such a short visit was out of character. He should probably get over to Jeff's and try to find out . . . he should probably—

He shrugged, inched a cigarette free from the pack in his

5

breast pocket and moved toward the foyer and the street. On the sidewalk he breathed in the warm summer night, then slumped in spine-to-shoulders recumbency against the polished granite buttress of the hotel entrance as he lit his cigarette. The street was quiet; at this hour the neighborhood was quiet. The Hotel Duarte was quiet, too, Johnny reflected; they could use a little business.

He half straightened from his drowsing introspection as a taxicab pulled into the curb in front of him. He flipped his cigarette out into the street and regretted it immediately when he saw that the cab was empty. He debated lighting another; it didn't seem worth the effort.

"You. You, there, bellhop."

Johnny focused reluctantly on the long visored baseball cap and the pointing finger extended in his direction from the cab. He grunted uncharitably but propelled himself from the supporting wall. He crossed the sidewalk in the swaying shuffle dictated by nature's overendowment of chest and shoulders, and his voice was a burred growl. "I'm listenin', Mac."

"You Johnny?" The baseball cap jerked a thumb back over its shoulder. "Woman wants to see you. Eight or ten doors up the street. She wouldn't let me bring her down here."

"Drunk?"

The lean features under the cap squinted appraisingly. "I don't—she's anyhow walking. Not makin' a hell of a lot of sense, though, maybe you're right."

"She pay you?"

"Yeah."

"I'll take care of it."

"It's all yours, chum." The cab pulled away and rolled west down Forty-fifth, and Johnny turned right and walked in the opposite direction, toward Sixth Avenue. In the light of the liquor store window next door to the hotel his bronzed, high-cheekboned face, rough yellow hair and pale, thick brows, frosty gray eyes and a nose that hooked left and right unexpectedly from unset breaks contributed to a hard-bitten effect.

He walked purposefully. It wouldn't be the first time a female guest had gazed upon wine too freely flowing and requested anonymous re-entry to her room. Must be someone who knew him, though, since they'd used his name. It was

6

pure hell handling a drunken woman; this would more than likely be a mess.

"Johnny!" He pulled up at the husky, low-voiced call; he'd passed her. Whoever it was had ducked in behind the wooden door to a sleazy upstairs rooming house. He tried to make out features in the pale blur that was all he could distinguish as he walked toward her; in the shadows of the doorway he had one lightning-like teasing tug from his sub-conscious, and then recognition burst upon him. It rocked him. "Ellen! What are *you* doing here?"

Her hand gripped his arm convulsively as he stared down at her. In the partial darkness he could see bare arms and shoulders shimmering above her dress; there was sudden movement in the crook of the arm held protectively across her body, and it took him a moment longer to identify the small, lightish blob silhouetted against her dress as a white kitten. He poked an inquiring finger at it, and the kitten hissed at him. "Who's the passenger, Ellen?"

She might never have heard him. "You've got to help me, Johnny!" She clung fiercely to his arm.

"Did I ever say no to that proposition, kid?" The huskiness in his voice surprised him; it hadn't come out sounding quite as flippant as he had intended. A long time ago—well, six or seven years ago—Ellen Saxon had been married to Johnny Killain. Temporarily. Two short years temporarily, he reminded himself. Yeah, and one of you has never gotten over it.

The hand on his arm tightened. "Hide me, Johnny. Please! Some place in the hotel. I've got to—think. Please, Johnny!"

"Hide you? What's spooked you, kid?"

He could hear the hysteria rising in her voice. "Please! Don't talk. Get me off the street. Please!"

He tried to see her face more clearly, but the shadows prevented it. He shrugged in the gloom; Ellen was really upset, and she wasn't the type to become upset easily. Well, one thing at a time. First get her settled down—he took her arm. "Let's go. I'll register you in and get—"

"No! No registering!" Panic soared in the so-well-remembered voice. "Please, Johnny! Just hide me!"

He didn't like it. There aren't too many crimes you can commit around a hotel more serious than slipping in an un-registered person. He opened his mouth, then closed it. She

7

was scared to death. Of somebody or something. She was scared, and she'd come to him. He drew her toward the side-walk. "I'll load you on the service elevator from the alley. Nobody'll see us."

"You're sure?" With her first step she crowded up against him, and a little shiver ran through him. Cut it out, he told himself impatiently; all that was dead and buried five years ago. But the little shiver paid no attention to what he told himself.

"Sure I'm sure. Come on." He could feel her reluctance to move from the shelter of the doorway, and he increased the pressure on her arm. "Let's go, kid." He noticed at once in the slightly better light on the sidewalk that her hair was different. Hell, in five years she'd probably had it cut five different ways. He'd liked it better the old way, though. He wondered if she remembered how she'd worn it then. How—

He only half heard the light squeal of brakes in the street behind them. He didn't begin to react until she had jerked free from his hand and backed away from him with the ridiculous kitten still on her arm and her mouth a little round O. He could see her throat swell suddenly, and her voice was a bugle in the upper register.

"Johnny—!"

The bugle blurted to a gargle as he slapped her firmly in the belly; she doubled and sat down like a well-oiled hinge. He was already on his way down to the sidewalk beside her when the four staccato reports went off behind him. Automatic, he told himself as he heard the splintering thud of the bullets in the rooming house's wooden door, and he rolled over to get his knees under him. He could see the dark sedan stopped right in the middle of the street. No sound from Ellen—no time to look. With thick rage a solid thing in his throat he surged up and charged the sedan.

A solitary brain cell registered the hasty rolling up of the front window on the driver's side an instant before Johnny rammed heavily against the door of the sedan. He grunted as he rebounded and smashed an impotent fist against the glass. He stooped, gripped the outer edge of the car frame and heaved mightily. The sedan rocked; Johnny bowed his back, and the motor roared. Tires screeched—he grabbed the door handle as he straightened, the sedan shot away from him with a rush of power and he was spun off into the street.

8

He rolled over twice and struck the curb with his shoulder. A flickering blackness deeper than the after-midnight street darkness hovered for an instant and then cleared. Ellen knelt beside him in the gutter, and her voice was an urgent contralto litany. "Johnny! Johnny! Johnny!"

He sat up dizzily. "All right, kid. Save it for when you need it." He tried to look up at her and found himself at eye level with the solemn, unblinking gaze of the white kitten still in the crook of Ellen's arm. He nodded approvingly. "You got the right idea, Whitey. Let's not get too shook over this little corrida." He heaved himself to his knees. "Come on, Ellen. No barricades out here if there should be a rebuttal." She took his arm anxiously.

On the sidewalk beside them a high-pitched voice spoke in the accents of age. "Craziest thing I ever seen, Jack. You tryin' to tip him over in the street?" He was a thin, elderly man with wispy gray hair, and he looked at Johnny as at some strange animal.

Johnny eased himself erect; it took an effort. Something seemed to be the matter with his right hand, and he looked down at it. He was still holding the door handle of the sedan; it took a little prying with his left hand to loosen it from his right palm, and it clattered into the gutter. He removed the jacket of his uniform, with a reminding twinge from his arm, and swung it over Ellen's bare shoulders; the white glow of her must be visible clear to Broadway, he thought.

"Holy Maria!" the high-pitched voice said in awed accents. "Tore the handle right offa the door. Right offa the damn—"

"Okay, Pop." Johnny looked hard at him. "Stop racin' your motor. Blow. Deal 'em somewheres else. Fly away home."

The elderly man backed off precipitately. "Yeah. Yeah, sure. Sure." He kept looking back over his shoulder.

They did not seem to have attracted too much other attention, Johnny reflected, which considering the neighborhood and the hour was not too surprising. That couldn't reasonably be expected to endure indefinitely, though; as he again started Ellen toward the hotel he strained mentally to get a reaction from his one quick glimpse of the dark, shapeless figure that had been huddled over the steering wheel of the sedan. He shook his head; he didn't even know if it had been man, woman, or child.

Ellen's pumps scuffed along beside him in the night mist on

9

the alley cobblestones. He led her through the big iron door that led into the hotel's subbasement and along the narrow fifteen-foot passageway to the elevator. In its light he got his first good look at her; Ellen's lipstick grimaced at him like a clown's mouth in the pallor of her face as she tried to smile at him. "Same old Johnny."

"Same old Ellen." Not really, though, he thought. The body that had been so youthfully promising had now spectacularly matured. Her dress did not hint at it; it stated it firmly. The eyes were the same—level, intelligent. Blue eyes that contrasted well with the dark hair and the duskily Indianized complexion. Her brows were black wings. He could see the indistinct tiny scar on the short upper lip, souvenir of a childhood accident. The tiny scar that appeared only when she was extremely fatigued or emotionally aroused. He remembered with a wrench the hours and the nights he had spent in provoking the appearance of the little scar; Ellen had always been a very generous person. Something seemed to ache dully behind his eyeballs. On Ellen's arm the kitten tongued a paw and transferred the paw to its small, serious face.

She spoke tiredly from the depths of her exhaustion. "You didn't have to do that, Johnny. Or this, either. I realize it now. I shouldn't have asked you. I have no right. I just panicked—"

He stopped her with a finger on her lips. "Some things don't change much, kid. Let's go upstairs."

Her voice was choked. "Johnny?"

"Skip it, Ellen." He extended a finger toward the kitten, and the white ruff around the small neck swelled angrily. "This kid is right on the muscle, isn't he? What's his name?"

"He's a she. A Persian. I'm delivering—I call her Sassy."

"Suits her." He tried to pin her eyes with his own, but she evaded him. "You gonna tell me now about this skirmish?"

He could see the flesh tighten over her cheekbones as her features set rigidly. She shook her head. "Not now. Please."

"Right now, lady. You think this is something to fool around with after what just happened outside?"

Her hand came up slowly in an effort to conceal the trembling of her lips. "Please, Johnny. I saw . . . I think I saw something—" She hesitated. "I'm not sure what I saw. I've got to think. I've—" Her body began to shake uncontrollably, and she moistened dry lips. "Let me rest a little, Johnny. Let me think. Then—then I'll talk to you . . . please."

10

He gave up. He would have to get her quieted down first; then he would get the whole story. He slid the shining bronze doors shut in a crash of metal, and the elevator ascended quietly.

CHAPTER 2

THE CUSTOMER ENTERED BRISKLY through the wide glass doors of Stone's and walked directly to the watch trays. The stout young clerk in the white linen jacket paused in his early morning task of removing the lightweight linen dustcloths from the showcases and moved in behind the counter. The subdued indirect fluorescent lighting, the lush, heavy carpeting, the elaborately simple individual displays and the ornate marble staircase winding away to the offices on the second floor all contributed to the cathedral-like serenity which was the hallmark of Stone's, Jewelers.

"Yes, sir?"

"You Manny Kessler? Tom Jenkins told me to look you up. Said you might have the Medallion in the Donada line."

Warmth came into the clerk's voice. "I'm Kessler, and we do have the Medallion, sir." Jenkins? Tom Jenkins? Manny Kessler couldn't remember a Tom Jenkins, but he had not the slightest trouble at all in remembering that the Medallion was the most expensive ladies' number in the line. He opened a drawer beneath the counter and removed a glistening minuscule watch which he displayed on the black velvet pad of the showcase. "An exceptional value, sir."

The customer picked up the watch and turned it over in his hands appraisingly.

"The very finest twenty-one jeweled movement, sir. And look at the styling. The very—"

"I'll take it."

Manny nodded, and turned immediately to pick up a gift box from the back counter. A bit disconcerting to have the animals walk in off the street and jerk the merchandise right out of your hand, but a sale is a sale. Never offer to

11

show them anything after they've pronounced the fatal words. Procrastination is the thief of commissions. "Charge, sir?"

"Cash." The customer fingered out four crisp new bills from a slim billfold. He picked up his wrapped package and a very small amount of change and left as rapidly as he had entered. Manny shrugged as he closed the register drawer. Not a bad start.

He moved back in the direction of the still jacketed showcases, then detoured to the front of the shop. Behind the front window he paused; he was concealed from the eyes of passers-by by the heavy, dove-gray drapery which served as a window backdrop. He moved a fold slightly to one side and looked across the street.

Sam was there.

Sam was standing just behind the front window of his store across the street. Watching. Just standing and watching, as he had yesterday, last week and last month. Standing and staring across the street. You didn't really even need to see him, Manny thought to himself. You can feel him.

He forced himself to move away from the window. Stop thinking about it, he told himself. You're getting as bad as he is. Forget about Sam. An ulcer you need? Sam would like that. Sam would like that fine, but ulcers are too good for what Sam would wish for Richard Harrison Stone, Jr.

He walked back to the showcases, but even as his hands deftly folded and creased and laid away his mind treacherously reverted to the front window of the store across the street. For the thousandth time he told himself wearily, will you cut it out? You hadn't been Sam's partner. Richard Harrison Stone, Jr. had been Sam's partner, and you didn't see Richard Harrison Stone, Jr. worrying about Sam.

Manny stared down unseeingly at a folded dust cloth. Richard Harrison Stone, Jr. had insisted that his former partner Sam buy him out. He had had a number of reasons, all of which Sam had sought to brush aside. Sam hadn't wanted to buy out his young partner; Sam had the money, all right, but he was satisfied with things as they were. Still, if your partner wants out, what can you do? Sam had called Sol, who had been his lawyer for twenty years, and Sol had drawn up the papers.

And three months later Richard Harrison Stone, Jr. had opened up across the street from Sam. Sam had just about

12

torn the front door off his safe getting out his reduction of partnership papers and had found out in a hurry that there was no restrictive clause. Found out, too, in the first hysterical telephone call that Sol had acquired a new client—Richard Harrison Stone, Jr.

Sam had found it out a little late, that was all. In business a man protects himself, or stands in windows looking across the street.

Manny looked up at the glass doors as they opened again, glad of the interruption. The fat man came directly to him, bluff and hearty, and thrust a magazine clipping into his hand.

"Need six of these," he said breezily. He grinned toothily. "Promotion job. Got to be identical. You fix me up?"

"Six?" Manny glanced down at the pictured Medallion. "Ah . . . six. Certainly. By two o'clock—"

"Not a chance, son." The fat man was emphatic as Manny again opened the drawer beneath the counter. "I'm due at a sales' meeting in twenty minutes. How many you got?"

"I have four. In an hour, even—"

"Any in the window?"

"Let me look." Manny knew there were no Medallions in the window, but he was following Precept Number Two of Richard Harrison Stone, Jr. Give the customer a little action for his money. Check the window. Check the vault. Check the wastebaskets. Check anything. Move. Look alive. Look like you want the business. "Sorry, sir. Not another one in the shop."

"Gimme the four." The fat man tossed a coarse handful of money on the counter top. "My girl'll have to shoot out and pick me up a couple while I stall 'em in the meeting."

Manny looked thoughtfully after the departing rotund figure. He rubbed his chin; sure must be some promotion. Steam shovels, at least. Or locomotives. He wished he'd had the other two Medallions. How could you figure this business? You might sell two a month, ordinarily. If you were lucky. Now here they had snatched five away from him in a morning. Morning? He glanced at his watch. Hell, in an hour.

He made a note on the "out" pad beside the register and looked up again as the glass doors parted majestically to admit Richard Harrison Stone, Jr. He watched the customary impressive entrance, inclining his own head in response to

13

the curt nod he received, and his eyes followed the dignified ascent of the lean, aristocratic figure to the second floor offices. Automatically Manny straightened the set of the white linen jacket across his shoulders. He disliked the jacket, but the jacket constituted Precept Number One of Richard Harrison Stone, Jr. A potential customer, the owner was fond of saying smugly and often, finds a certain psychological block in dealing for a piece of expensive merchandise with a man better dressed than himself. Therefore a clerk should look like a clerk. Like a white-linen-jacketed clerk.

Manny glanced back at the door as the morning's first customer re-entered the shop in a shambling trot and plowed toward him. The man's face was flushed, and he was obviously repressing emotion. He slapped down on the counter the wrapped package that Manny had given him.

"Like to return this," he said carefully in a hoarse, strained voice. He tried to smile. "She wouldn't even look at it. Or at me."

"Sorry," Manny murmured. "It happens." He toed the buzzer which would bring Max out from his watchmaking cubicle. Manny took his time making out the refund slip; beside him Max unobtrusively opened the package, looked carefully at the watch, checked the itemization on the refund slip, and silently returned the watch to the drawer beneath the counter. You never knew, Manny reflected. Even in a shop like this you could find someone trying a switch. It was never any problem, though; on a return you just called Max.

The girl must really have given this boy a hard time, Manny thought as he made the refund and the unhappy gentleman departed. A woman-hater, till the next time. He glanced at his watch again. Eleven. Slow morning.

And as though linked by an invisible wire he drifted down the counter and out to the front window, where he again lifted a fold of the drapery and looked across the street. Bright sunlight reflected from Sam's window and dazzled him. He dropped the drapery. So you can't see, Kessler. You need to see? Sam is standing there. Watching. Waiting.

Manny's full lips twitched. Sam was mad at Stone, all right; Sam was purely out-of-his-mind mad at Stone, but Sam was mad at Manny, too. Manny had worked for Sam, before and after the breakup of the partnership. And then Stone had come after Manny and made him a very, very good offer. Sam would have matched it, of course. Sam would have

14

screamed like a stuck whistle on the Staten Island ferry, but he would have matched it. Sam had liked Manny. Manny had kind of liked Sam, too, but he hadn't given Sam a chance to match the offer. Are you a fool, Kessler? he had asked himself. Look at them. Look at Sam's place, and look at Stone's. All right, Stone's a gonnif, but he's going places. His money spends. Manny had gone with Stone.

On quiet mornings like this he sometimes wondered about that decision. Not that Sam could do anything. Not that—

He turned at the sound of the doors and looked at the overdressed blonde pushing her way inside. She was followed by a man in a dark suit, and both of them by a big man in a rich-looking sport coat and light-colored slacks. The big man wore an expensive panama with a too-wide brim, and he had a livid scar that pulled down a corner of the heavy mouth slightly.

Manny looked at the blonde, and a little warning bell jangled in his mind. Sometimes you got a feeling. A beef— even here you had to get one once in a while. The blonde looked in Manny's direction and pointed. He sighed; it figured.

"That the one?" the big man demanded. His voice was fantastically deep. You surely should be able to hear him a quarter mile upwind in a storm, Manny thought. The voice rumbled at him as the big man advanced upon the counter. "You, there." He dangled a watch suspended from a bracelet in Manny's face. "You sold my girl a phony watch. Don't try to deny it."

"If I might just see the watch," Manny said in his patiently courteous voice, "I might not have to deny it."

"Here." The big man thrust it at him. "Lost thirty minutes every day she's had it, and—"

"Occasionally even a new one needs an adjustment," Manny wedged into the roar of the waterfall. He looked at the watch—a Medallion. Another Medallion. He looked at the blonde and remembered. She had bought it last week. On Medallions this morning they were in a rut so deep it was a trench. He turned back to the big man. "If you will kindly permit our watchmaker to—"

"Will you listen to me?" He had never heard such a voice, Manny thought. If crystalware had been on display, it would surely have been shattered by now. "I know they need adjusting sometimes. When Nora told me she was having

15

trouble with it I thought I'd save her a trip across town. Took it to my own man, and when he looked at it he said it's got a movement he can buy for two dollars and a half."

"Impossible," Manny said at once. He made sure that his voice was polite but firm. He toed the buzzer for Max and handed over the watch when the stooped little watchmaker appeared. Max fumbled uneasily with his leather apron; he always looked uncomfortable in the front of the shop. He listened to Manny's quick explanation, automatically inserted his loupe in his eye and delicately unscrewed the back of the case. His head came up at once.

"The watch came from here?" he asked carefully, and the blonde fumbled in her bag and produced a sales' slip which she waved at him.

"I remember the sale," Manny said. He thought that his voice sounded a little faint; he tried to strengthen it. "Distinctly."

Max cleared his throat. "It is not a Medallion movement."

Manny stared at him, and the man in the dark suit spoke for the first time. Manny observed now that he had a hard, authoritative face. "You got any more of these watches here?"

"No," Manny began, then remembered the lovelorn suitor. "Wait. We do have." He opened the drawer. "Here."

"Open it up," the man in the dark suit said to Max. His tone was brusque. Manny found himself leaning forward on tiptoe to see more clearly, and when the back came off the case and he saw the look on Max's usually stolid features he felt as though his own stomach had turned over.

The man had seen the look, too. He took both watches back from Max and removed from his pocket a leather billfold, which he opened. Manny caught the flash of metal.

"D.A.'s Racket Squad," the man said curtly. "You the owner here?"

Automatically Manny's eyes went aloft. "No. Mr. Stone—"

"Let's all go upstairs and see Mr. Stone, boys."

16

J OHNNY GLANCED AT THE CLOCK over the bell captain's desk in the recessed niche between the elevators as he emerged into the semi-darkened lobby. Five after three. He crossed directly to the marbled registration desk.

His final try upstairs had been unable to get a word out of Ellen. She had sunk bonelessly upon the bed in the room to which he had taken her and had turned her face to the wall. Please, she had said in reply to all his prodding. Please. Not now. Let me rest. Let me think. Please.

A hundred irritated questions had crowded up behind his teeth, but he had kept the teeth locked. Let her settle down. It had better be soon, though; whatever it was that had scared her was no damn joke. Four slugs in the door against which they'd been standing was no joke at all.

He leaned over the registration counter, craning to look for Vic Barnes, the night front-desk man. He slapped an open palm down on the smooth surface. "Vic!"

"Yo, John." Vic ambled up from behind the cashier's wicket, threading his way along the narrow aisle which separated the rear of the counter from the mail rack. He looked at Johnny inquiringly. Vic was a stocky, middle-aged man in a clerk's black alpaca jacket; he had a smooth, round face and pink cheeks with a glossy sheen upon the skin that made it seem waxed. He had sparse sandy hair rapidly turning gray, combed straight back from a high forehead, and he wore steel-rimmed spectacles low on the bridge of his nose. It was an easygoing face; Vic was an easygoing man.

"Couldn't see you back there," Johnny told him. "Listen. Block out 629 for me."

Vic pursed full lips. "Fun and games again? When you gonna grow up, John?" He shook his head doubtfully, but he was already reaching for the room rack, pencil in hand.

"I'll have her out of there by daylight. Are we going fish-

17

ing Thursday morning with Mike? He's already asked me three times."

"Tell him yes, then," Vic replied promptly. "It's his gas he's going to burn." He reached for his phone as it rang. "Front desk, Barnes. Oh, hello there. Still up? You should —who? Why, no, I don't—"

Johnny turned away and walked back to his bell-captain's desk. He removed his big flashlight from the lower drawer and re-crossed the lobby to the telephone switchboard at the far end of the registration desk. He leaned his elbows on the little gate that set the board off from the lobby proper and looked in at Sally Fontaine, its headphoned night operator. "Hi, Ma."

His voice brought her head up, and she smiled out at him. She nodded at the light in his hand. "Prowling again?"

"Yeah. Paul go out?"

"Just for coffee."

"Tell him where he can find me when he gets back."

She inclined her head as the board buzzed. She pulled a plug and the buzzing stopped, and she looked out at him again. She was a small girl, almost painfully thin. She might have been thirty. Her nose was short and tiptilted, and her brown hair was an indeterminate shade very nearly justifying the adjective mousy. The brown eyes and the too generous mouth smiled easily and warmly.

Johnny spoke softly into the lobby's hush. "You comin' up in the mornin', Ma? Business meetin'."

"A likely story, Johnny Killain."

"Surest thing you ever heard. Business meetin' to consider the settin' up of a joint venture, the deal open only to the subscribin' partners." He grinned at her. "Who're you 'n me. You a customer?"

"Any capital required?"

"You're totin' your assets, kid."

"I am? What's the valuation?"

"The assessor's report isn't in yet, but I got a feelin' it's high grade ore. You gonna see me in the mornin', Ma?"

She smiled, and the severe planes of the narrow face lightened remarkably. She looked like a different person. "A girl could get a reputation, seeing you in the mornings."

"She could earn it, too."

"You don't seem to manage your business affairs very discreetly. With a new manager around here—"

18

"Hell with him. You be there."

She smiled again, and waved as he turned. He walked across to the wide flight of marbled stairs leading up to the mezzanine and started up. The hotel had a night watchman, but he was not a hotel employee; he was from a protective association, and he had other stops in the block. Years ago Johnny had formed the habit of making a swing himself around the mezzanine and the ground floor, usually around three in the morning when things had quieted down. Once in a while a drunk fell asleep upstairs in the lounge, or one of the stores on the mezzanine forgot to lock up at closing time.

It was not a large hotel; four hundred and twenty-five rooms, give or take a few always in the process of redecoration. It was not a new hotel; a slightly shabby comfort had its own attraction for a number of people who preferred a certain quiet dullness to a bright and shining newness with its accompanying sharp edges. The hotel was understaffed, like most such, particularly on the night side. Johnny, Vic, Paul, and Sally had had it to themselves as a regular crew for seven or eight years, with occasional and inconsequential help from part-time bellboys and elevator operators.

A good many years ago it had been a first-class hotel, but the neighborhood had changed and the theatrical people who had once patronized it extensively had now moved across Broadway. Because of its midtown location it still had a steady businessman clientele and a number of permanents, some of whom had been there for years.

Johnny swung up on the landing, past the executive offices, and turned right. He hurried as he swept the bulls'-eye flash around the dim shadows of the interior lounge; he wanted to get back upstairs. He could easily hear the echoing sound of his heels in the quiet as he walked down the far side of the mezzanine and tried the doors of the travel bureau, the barber shop, the beauty shop, the haberdashery, the theatre ticket agency and the public stenographer's office. Satisfied, he descended the same flight of stairs to the main floor lobby and cut back underneath through the muraled swinging doors which led into the bar, dark except for the night light.

He walked down its long expanse and removed a key from a clip on the band of his wrist watch. He unlocked the

19

door at the far end of the bar leading into the kitchen and, flashlight in hand, made a quick circuit of the cavernously gloomy area whose long stainless-steel counters sprang to glistening life under the probing beam of the light. He tried the fire door at the back end of the huge room, the padlocked doors on the walk-in boxes and the hooked catches on the windows, and returning to his starting point let himself out and re-locked the door.

Back in the lobby he returned to the registration desk and found Paul behind it, idly turning the pages of the early edition. "Vic go out? How soon's he due back?"

"Any time." Paul glanced at his watch. "He's a little overdue right now. Another couple of minutes, probably."

Johnny hesitated, and Paul looked at him inquiringly. Paul, the elevator operator, was a slender man, four or five years older than Johnny's thirty-five; his hair was dark and slicked down closely to a small skull. He had a stolid, unimaginative face, but a firm mouth and chin; Paul was reliable. "I want you to cover for me," Johnny explained. "I need to run upstairs a few minutes."

"So go ahead," Paul said at once, folding up his paper. "Vic'll be back in a minute. I'm not likely to get any conventions to check in till he gets here."

"It's quiet enough," Johnny agreed. "Okay. If you need me ring 629. It's not on the board."

Paul nodded. As he turned away from the desk Johnny reflected that one of Paul's primary virtues was that he needed no diagrams.

Johnny stepped out into the sixth-floor corridor after anchoring the cab of the service elevator with a slab of wood, and a flash of white at the end of the hall caught his eye. He looked more closely and discovered a white kitten galloping in spurting dashes, twin white paws batting at a dustball.

"What the hell?" Johnny was surprised to find that he had said it aloud. There couldn't be two white kittens in this place. Not on the sixth floor, anyway. This kitten should have been behind the door of 629, and since it wasn't something was wrong.

He advanced on the kitten, which wheeled to confront him. When Johnny was half a dozen paces away the small back arched slowly, and the white fur seemed to swell enormously, especially around the neck. A long, surprisingly loud hiss accompanied this display of defiance, and Johnny

20

laughed as he dropped to his knees. "You need a new matchmaker, white stuff; you're givin' away too much weight." He extended a finger, slowly and steadily, and the kitten watched its approach, eyes of an unexpectedly bright blue fearlessly studying the problem. Johnny ran the finger right up to the ridiculous whiskers, and in movement too quick to follow the kitten turned its head and seized the finger in its mouth.

It was not a bite; Johnny could feel the impression of the needle-like little fangs, but he knew it was just a holding action while the kitten debated the seriousness of the assault. With his left hand he scooped up the small body, and the fangs closed down. Johnny stood up and worked his finger free, and he and Sassy looked down at the two bright drops of blood which dotted its surface. "Okay, tiger; you won a battle, but you lost the war. It's happened to heavyweights. Now let's go see how you got out here."

With the kitten riding his arm he turned back down the corridor to 629. He could see that the door was tightly closed as he approached it, and his feeling of unease increased. He couldn't imagine Ellen Saxon opening the door of that room to anyone in the mood in which he had left her, yet somehow the kitten had gotten out into the hall.

At the door he fumbled for his pass key. Then the door opened inward suddenly as he reached for the lock, and Vic Barnes stood teetering on the threshold, breast-to-breast with Johnny.

Vic's face was ghastly, perspiration streamed down the faded, round cheeks, and the eyes were all whites. Vic's mouth opened convulsively, but no sound emerged; he half turned to look back over his shoulder, and rubberlegged a sideways step as Johnny impatiently pushed past him and inside.

A stride beyond the door he stopped in his tracks.

Ellen Saxon lay on the bed where he had left her; for a long moment Johnny stared in disbelief at the twisted limbs, the outflung arm with which she had sought in vain to protect herself, the so-well-remembered face that was now a death mask of horror. A puffed, blue, strangulated horror.

He drew a harsh breath and crossed the room in a lunge. He felt for a pulse and dropped the limp wrist hopelessly. There was no pulse. Ellen—he still couldn't believe it.

He fought his way back up to the surface; he couldn't

21

seem to get off dead center mentally. He forced himself to lean forward and look more closely at Ellen's outthrust arm and hand; he avoided looking at her face. When he turned to Vic he didn't recognize his own voice. "What were you doing up here, Vic?"

Vic never even heard him. The stocky man had dropped down on a chair just inside the door and had retreated to a private world of his own. He was bent nearly double in the chair, with the lower half of his face cradled in his hands and the protruding eyes staring glassily.

Johnny stepped into the bathroom and turned on the cold water. He grabbed a towel from the rack, soaked it in the running water, wrung it out hard, folded it three times lengthwise and brought it out and handed it to Vic, who plunged his face into it. Johnny was already making the round trip to wet down another towel; by the third trip Vic was back on his feet and Johnny had a hand on his shoulder. "Why did you come up here, Vic?"

The waxen-faced man swallowed hard. A hand crept up and removed his glasses, absently stuffing them into the breast pocket of his jacket. He had trouble finding his voice; it seemed to come from a long distance. "I—I can't tell you."

"What the hell do you mean you can't tell me!" Johnny rapped back at him. Without the glasses the deathly pale features looked more defenseless than before. He looked at the water marks from the wet towels on the shoulders of the black alpaca jacket, and he tried to keep his voice down. "Look, Vic; this is Johnny. I don't think you did it. I know you better than that. I know you didn't do it, but I also need to know a few other things. Why did you come up here?"

Vic stared at him dumbly.

Johnny fought for patience. "How much time you think we got, Vic? This is important. I've worked with you for seven years. Fifty times I've asked you to block out a room for me. This is the first time you ever came upstairs. Why?"

The stocky man's voice was a leaden monotone. "The p-police will say I did it."

It brought Johnny up short. They would, too, if Vic didn't make any more sense than he had up to now. If they don't think *you* did it, he added silently to himself. He had to find out what Vic knew before the police got there, or he wasn't going to find out anything at all.

He pushed Vic back down into the chair again, and the

22

spaniel eyes stared up at him. "Are you listening, Vic? Do you hear me?"

A nod, and again the hard swallowing movement of the throat.

"The police are going to ask you the same thing I did, Vic." Johnny leaned over him. "What are you going to tell them?"

Silence. And then Vic's head came up, and a fleeting impression of an expression passed over the damp, ashen face. "I'll tell them—" He hesitated, and his voice strengthened a little with the necessity for conveying his thought. "I'll tell them I—had a date with her. Yes. Date with her . . . that's it."

Johnny restrained a wild desire to laugh. "Date with her? You? For God's sake, Vic—"

But Vic had gone away again. With the head bowed the slack-lipped mumble was scarcely understandable. "—date with her."

Johnny's nails bit into his palms. Time. No time. No time for this damned foolishness. Somewhere inside him a spring was winding down, tighter and tighter. He leaned forward again. "Vic!" He tried to put his own desperate sense of urgency into his voice. "You know they're gonna take you in if you tell them that?" He stared down at Vic's bowed head; he wasn't getting through. He aimed his hard voice down at the withdrawn man. "Do you know who she was, Vic?"

And Vic's head came up; again the voice was a little stronger. "Yes. Ellen Saxon."

Johnny felt winded, suspended in space and time. How did Vic know Ellen Saxon? How had he known she was here in this room? How did— He shook his head. No time. No time at all. He tried to capitalize on the breakthrough. "Vic. Look at me. Did you know that Ellen Saxon had been married to me?"

The whites overran Vic's eyes. "Mar—ried?" The halting voice made two distinct syllables of the one word; before Johnny's eyes the bones of the round face seemed to dissolve, and the facial flesh slackened. The stocky man pitched sideways from his chair, and Johnny had to lunge hard to catch him before he hit the floor.

The jolting grab as his arms absorbed Vic's weight released Johnny from his own inertia. He lifted strongly, settling Vic back in the chair and propping him up. He

23

glanced quickly around the room; he had a lot to do, and he wasn't thinking clearly.

He grabbed up his torn uniform jacket from the floor, the jacket he had thrown over Ellen's shoulders out in the street in that short time ago that now seemed like such a long time ago. He scooped up the wet towels, and looked for the kitten. He picked up the small white body from the floor where it was playing with the tassels on the bedspread and tucked it under his arm.

In the corridor a dozen strides took him to the door of 615, his own room. He opened it, dropped jacket, towels, and kitten inside, and closed and locked it. Back at the door of 629 he saw that Vic was again in the land of the living, and his voice was hard. "On your feet, Vic. Got to get out of here."

In the doorway, with Vic already in the corridor, Johnny stopped and turned for a final searing look at the bed. Repressed emotion rioted within him, but he held it down. Savagely he closed the door from the outside and propelled Vic down the hall. Vic moved like an automaton, with Johnny's hand at his elbow.

They moved like a team off the elevator into the lobby, and Paul looked up from the registration desk. "You found him. I was beginning—" Paul broke off when he saw Johnny's face. His glance slid off to Vic, hesitated, and returned to Johnny.

"Got a bad one, Paul," Johnny told him. He glanced around the deserted lobby. "Get Sally up here. We got work to do."

Paul silently slithered down the narrow passageway behind the marbled counter and was back almost immediately with Sally. She looked from Johnny to Vic, and her thin features turned anxious.

"All right," Johnny said abruptly. He tried to sort out his thoughts. "Listen close; I only got time to say this once. We have a dead woman up in 629. Her name is Ellen Saxon. She used to be—"

"Oh, Johnny, no!" Sally's shocked exclamation halted his staccato recital. "Ellen? Dead?"

"Murdered." The word seemed to reverberate through the stillness of the lobby. "She used to be my wife," he explained to Paul. No need to explain to Sally. Sally was the one person in the world who knew how Johnny Killain had felt about

24

Ellen Saxon. "I put her in the room about an hour ago, unregistered. Vic found her there about fifteen minutes ago. Approximately."

Sally's hand was at her throat. "Oh, Johnny—"

He continued harshly. "We're going to cut our losses a little before we call the police. We'll register her in, now. Gimme a blank, Paul."

He took the registration card and handed it to Sally. "Need a woman's handwriting. Put down 'Ellen Saxon'."

She wrote swiftly, and looked up at him. "Address?"

Johnny grunted. Address? That was a bad one. He didn't know. Where—

"Four Twelve Darby Court." Johnny's eyes swiveled to Vic, who had said it. You couldn't tell from looking at that sodden, wrung-out face that Vic had said anything at all, Johnny reflected. Vic looked back at him, but it was a question if he saw him.

"Put it down," Johnny told Sally. "I don't know if it's right or not. I don't know how he knows, if it is. I don't know why he went up there. There's too damn much I don't know. Put it down. Paul?"

"Yes, Johnny?"

"Get me the logbook. And your screwdriver." He picked up the little screwdriver Paul laid down on the counter before he moved out from behind it and reached for the cord on the electric time clock. He pulled the plug, unfastened the two screws that held the metal cover in place on the clock, and slid it off. He turned to Paul at his elbow with the chronological listing of roomings and room service in the logbook and opened it to the current page. He almost smiled. "First break we've had tonight. Only half a dozen entries on this page, and they're all on this shift. Paul, you get this page out of here completely, and be careful no one can tell a page has been removed. On the new page write back in again the entries that were in your handwriting, leaving spaces for me to do the same. Leave me one extra space at the right place for me to enter Ellen Saxon as roomed at two-forty-five A.M. Got it?"

"Got it." Paul's tone was brisk; he was already slipping his knife from his pocket.

Johnny turned back to the time clock. With the speed born of practice he jiggered the dial with his screwdriver and set it back for a 2:38 A.M. punch, plugged the clock back in and

25

punched the back of the card Sally had filled out. He handed it to her. "Fix up the room carbons for this rack and yours, huh?" He could hear her at the typewriter as he unplugged the time clock again, reset it correctly after a glance at his watch and tested it with a blank card. He nodded, tore up the card, slid the metal cover back on and screwed it down tightly. On a bet one time he had done the whole thing in four minutes.

Paul pushed the logbook over to him, and Johnny reached for his pen. He looked across the counter at Sally. "All set? Call the police, and put Paul through to them. Paul, you say I just called you from upstairs."

Sally's features looked pinched. "What are you going to tell them?"

Johnny shrugged. "The truth, except this little corner we just cut here. I'd rather tell them I found her, but look at Vic. How long d'you think it would stand up once they started to talk to him?" He could see them looking at Vic, then quickly away. "The hell of it is they're a cinch to take him in." He picked up his pen again and started to write, then paused as he looked up. "Paul, after you talk to the police call in a couple of the boys that live closest. Get 'em in here fast. We're gonna have the law kneelin' on our chests the balance of this shift, and we'll need a little extra help till the day crowd comes on."

Sally moved down to the switchboard, and Paul again circled behind the counter and picked up his phone. Vic stood, motionless, and stared off into space. Johnny made the last entry in the logbook, closed it and returned it to the bell captain's desk. He ran back over the routine in his mind—that should do it. Ellen Saxon could now properly be accounted for so far as the hotel and the police were concerned, and he would not be held up by tedious executive office and police inquiries about a registry irregularity in his own effort to find the murderer of Ellen Saxon.

He drew a deep breath, and his hands clenched. He felt as though he had been running down a long, dark street. He looked down at his hands, and with an awkward movement forcibly relaxed their knotted rigidity. He turned away from the desk.

Paul was hanging up his phone as Johnny returned to him. "Okay?" Paul nodded silently. "Good. Keep an eye on the switchboard a few minutes, will you? I need to talk to Sally."

26

He continued on down to the little gate. "Let's go upstairs a minute, Ma. You might have the answers to a coupla questions I need answered."

She slipped off the headphone and stood up. He held the gate open for her and followed her across the lobby onto the service elevator. "Johnny—" she began tentatively, and he shook his head.

"Post mortems upstairs, Ma," he said, and his mouth twisted at the unintentional double entendre. He shot the cab aloft in a silent rush.

CHAPTER 4

JOHNNY CLOSED THE DOOR of his room behind them, and Sassy advanced from under the bed in a ludicrously stiff-legged prance, the small ears alertly cocked.

Sally stared. "Johnny! Where on earth—"

Johnny introduced them. "Sassy, this is Sally." He sat down in his armchair as Sally knelt and reached out a hand and drew the kitten to her. Sassy eyed her carefully, but made no protest, and Johnny shook his head. "How the hell do you like that? She like to ate me, horns and all, the first time I went near her."

"You're beautiful," Sally crooned to the kitten, and Sassy's head bobbed in complaisant agreement as she busily rough-tongued Sally's bare forearm. "Did you say 'her'?"

"Yeah. She's my new bodyguard."

"Where did you get her, Johnny?"

"Ellen."

"Oh." Reminded, Sally shivered. She put Sassy down and sat down on the arm of Johnny's chair. "I still can hardly —believe it. Why Ellen?"

"I've got some better 'whys' than that." Johnny stared across the room morosely. "Why did Ellen come here at all? Why wouldn't she tell me why she was so scared? Why did Vic go up to that room? Why can't I get it through my thick skull how the murderer could find her in an unregistered room?" He crouched forward in the chair, feeling driven in his impotence, then snorted impatiently and sank back. "Fix me a drink, Ma. Somethin's got to start the wheels turnin'."

"Do you think you should?" she asked doubtfully. "You've got to talk to the police, you know." She rose resignedly, however, and went to the wall cabinet and took down a bottle of bourbon and two three-finger shot glasses. She made a little face and returned one of them. "Why you can't use a civilized glass like ordinary people instead of these ten gallon hats you have here—"

"A slight exaggeration, Ma," he told her as she poured. "An' bring the bottle back here with you."

He accepted the brimming shot glass from her and tossed it off in a long, hard swallow. He waited for the impact, shuddered, took the bourbon bottle from Sally's hand and splashed a thimbleful more into the glass and chased the first load down. He refilled the shot glass again, and set glass and bottle down on the table beside the chair.

Sally broke the little silence. Her voice was quiet, but there was a note of constraint in it. "I realize how this must have shaken you, Johnny."

"Shaken me?" His lips drew back mirthlessly from his teeth. He picked up the refilled shot glass and gulped half its contents, then looked up at Sally on the arm of his chair. "You're the only one in the world who knew how I felt about that kid. I never blamed her for rackin' up on me when she did. I was a hard rock still livin' too close to those days overseas, an' she just couldn't understand. I hadn't seen her three times in the last five years, but it wasn't ever any different with me."

He stared down moodily into the half empty glass, lifted it suddenly and drained it. His hand closed tightly around the solid-feeling thickness of the glass, and his voice hoarsened. "So tonight she's in some kind of trouble, and she comes to me. To me, mind you. And what do I do for her? I get her killed." He bounded to his feet from the depths of the chair, furiously driven by the impotent anger bubbling in his veins, and his voice soared. "I'll tell you one thing. I'll find the guy that did it if I have to live to be a hundred and four. I'll get him. For sure I'll get him, and when I do I'll feed him to the crows a very small piece at a time. I'll get him, damn him—"

28

He whirled on the balls of his feet, and Sally gasped and smothered a scream as his arm rose and fell in a whiplash motion. The heavy shot glass exploded in a starburst of glass fragments in the center of the big dresser mirror, which vanished in a crystal spray. Johnny stood, half-crouched forward from the violence of his follow-through, his ears still filled with the soul-satisfying smash.

He straightened slowly; on the arm of the chair Sally was crying. He patted her head awkwardly, then walked over to the wall cabinet and removed the other shot glass. Back at the chair he poured himself another drink, the bourbon sloshing over the glass rim and running down his wrist and fingers.

"You'll be supposed to make s-sense when you talk to the police," Sally said disapprovingly, swiping at her eyes with the back of her hand.

"Make as much sense as usual." The phone rang, and he reached for it. "Yeah?"

"They're on the way up, Johnny."

"Thanks, Paul." He replaced the phone, looked at Sally and tried not to see the tear-streaks. "The constabulary, Ma. You got to run."

She scrubbed openly at her eyes with her hands, stood up and walked to the door. "Promise me you'll keep your temper, Johnny?"

"Yeah, yeah, Ma. Sure." He closed the door behind her and looked around the room. He picked Sassy up and carried her into the bathroom; he put her down in the tub as she blinked her disapproval. He closed the bathroom door and returned to the chair and his refilled glass. He sat down again and waited.

Trailing fingers of blue smoke swirled and drifted about the walls of his room; he sat and tested in his mind the cumulative questions and answers of the past two hours. He was tired of questions and answers. He looked at the eddying haze in the room; he ought to stir himself and open a window, he supposed. He sat where he was.

He looked up sharply as his door opened and the smoke gusted violently; Detective Cuneo walked directly to the straight-backed chair in the room's center and sat down astraddle it, facing front-to-back. His folded arms rested upon the upper back rest, and his chin rested upon his arms.

After two hours Johnny felt that he knew this man rather well. A quick, incisive man; a lean six-footer with a hatchet face and large-pupilled eyes. The mouth was snug and the lips thin; the jawline slanted to a sharp chin. Detective Cuneo entering a room looked like a detective entering a room.

"About Barnes—" the man in the chair said abruptly, and Johnny looked at him. "We're taking him in. He doesn't talk here maybe he'll talk over there."

"He didn't do it," Johnny said.

"I didn't say he did," Cuneo replied sharply. "I do say that he's not telling us what he knows. When he does—" He broke off as the door opened again, and he twisted to look at the slender, sandy-haired man who entered the room and closed the door again. "Hi, Jimmy. How'd you make out?"

"Tell you later." The slender man nodded to Johnny in his chair. " 'Lo, Johnny. Long time."

Johnny nodded in turn, and Cuneo looked from his partner to Johnny and back again. He couldn't keep the surprise from his voice. "You know this guy?"

"Tell you about that later, too. What's with you here?"

"I'm taking Barnes in. Completely unco-operative." He glanced back at Johnny. "I was just getting instructed here that Barnes didn't do it." He leaned forward over the back of the chair as the large-pupilled eyes glinted. "What makes you so sure, Killain?"

"You know why I'm sure. Ellen Saxon has a quarter pound of hair and skin under her fingernails, and there isn't even a pimple nicked on Vic. That lets him out."

"It lets him out of a first degree charge, maybe," Cuneo said sourly. "I still want the answers to some questions before he's out, period." He looked at Johnny. "How about you, Killain? Take your shirt off."

Johnny stood up slowly. "That's what I like about you types. Not 'Do you mind taking your shirt off, citizen?' Just 'Take it off'."

The hatchet face regarded him impassively. "You don't have to like it. Just do it."

"Sure you don't want to call in any witnesses? So I can't say I got scratched up while you were wrestlin' the shirt off me?"

30

Two red spots glowed dully in Cuneo's lean face. He looked, tight-lipped, at his partner, Jimmy Rogers. "Your friend's a character, I see." He swung back to Johnny. "Personally, I can do without all the conversation. Get it off!"

Johnny slipped out of his uniform jacket and removed tie, shirt, and T-shirt.

"Over here. Under the light." Cuneo's voice was taut.

Johnny crossed the room, and the detective looked him up and down. "The bear that walks like a man," he said grudgingly. "You get your shirts from a sailmaker?" His knuckles thumped lightly on Johnny's chest. "Quite a rug. What's this?" An inquiring finger probed in turn each of three dimpled indentations scarcely visible under the curling hair.

Johnny looked down at the finger. "There was this guy that didn't like me."

Cuneo grunted. "Looks like he didn't like you about three times with a thirty-eight. So?"

"So I reached him. He still doesn't like me."

The hatchet features stiffened. "I asked you what happened!"

A faint glow began to heat Johnny's interior. "It have anything to do with what happened in Room 629?"

Scarlet flooded Cuneo's face. "Are you refusing to answer?"

"I've answered for two hours. Did you ask any sensible questions you didn't get answered?"

"Killain, you'll answer what I ask you. I'll—"

"I'll answer what I damn please," Johnny interrupted. The faint glow flared to an open flame. He leaned forward slightly. "Do me a favor, boy scout. Drop dead."

The tall man crouched, but Jimmy Rogers spoke quickly. "Easy, Ted. He'd like that. I know this boy."

The dull red spots again emblazoned the pallor which had replaced Cuneo's high color. He bit his words off viciously. "If you know what's good for you you'll answer anything I ask you, Killain!"

"The hell I will. Go make your funny noises some place else."

The lean man took a short step forward and hesitated. His tongue circled his lips almost hungrily. Jimmy Rogers moved in front of his partner and nodded at Johnny's clothes on the bed. "Button it up, Johnny. Put your

31

clothes on, and we'll go down to the morgue and make the identification."

Johnny drew a deep breath. "No."

Cuneo charged back to the assault. "No? What the hell you mean, 'no'?"

"Anything the matter with your ears?"

"Listen, Killain—" Cuneo began dangerously, and Johnny cut him short.

"You listen to me for a change. You got all the identification from me you're gonna get. You know who she is."

Jimmy Rogers' voice was patient. "We're talking about the legal, positive identification by the next-of-kin downtown at—"

"So go get her next-of-kin."

"You're her husband!" Cuneo barked.

"Her ex-husband. No next-of-kin."

Cuneo looked at Rogers, who shrugged, and the tall man turned back uncertainly to Johnny. "You might have to convince the D.A."

"Send him around."

Cuneo glared. "Let's take him down there anyway, Jimmy," he suggested to his partner. He smiled. "The big buffalo acts like he thinks we couldn't do it."

Johnny looked at him. "I'll give you a written contract you won't enjoy it, buster."

Rogers cut in again quickly before his partner could speak. "You have to keep crowding, Johnny? There's an easier way. We know she was your wife. Maybe you got a right to be a little redheaded; on the other hand, your attitude wins no kewpie dolls."

"You can't sweet-talk his kind, Jimmy," Cuneo said tartly. "I've seen these fourteen-karat cop fighters before. Come on; let's get out of here." He stared, narrow-eyed, at Johnny. "I'll see you later, wise guy. Don't you even think of leaving the jurisdiction." He stamped out the door, and after a moment in which he seemed to be searching for an exit line Jimmy Rogers nodded slowly and followed suit.

Johnny stretched leisurely. He crossed to a window and opened it, and then turned to his clothes. He watched the blue haze thin out as he dressed, his mind still on Detective Ted Cuneo. Childish, he told himself. You, Killain; you're childish. From him you can get nothing but the worst of it, and still you have to needle him. You're the featherweight champion of the world in the brains department.

He retrieved Sassy from the bathroom and dropped her on the bed. He rubbed her lightly between the furry ears and teased the pink nose with a blunt fingertip. Sassy grabbed the finger in her small mouth, and Johnny laughed and then sobered. "I can take a hint, white stuff. We've got to get you straightened out in the grocery department. I'll run down to the kitchen and see what's on the menu. You take a white wine with your fish?"

Back on the service elevator he stopped the car at the mezzanine. He intended to walk down the final flight of stairs and cut back under them through the bar to the kitchen, but even before he had the cab door propped open he could hear the voices in the conversation coming up to him from the lobby below.

"—say you do know her, Mike?" Cuneo was saying.

"Sure I know her, Ted." The voice was pleasantly well-timbred. Johnny drifted forward silently to the front of the mezzanine. By leaning forward slightly he could see the three men in the lobby below him, a little back from the projecting edge of the balcony. He straightened; he didn't want to be seen because he wanted to hear. His one quick glance had taken in Cuneo and Rogers; the third man was Mike Larsen, a broad-shouldered husky with dark, wavy hair. Even in the stagnant heat of the early morning he was dressed neatly in slacks, a long-sleeved sport shirt with a button-down collar and a carefully knotted tie. Mike Larsen was a permanent at the hotel, a free-lance newspaperman who did special articles, and he was a friend of Vic's and Johnny's. Mike Larsen sounded disturbed.

"—tell me what's going on around here?" he was asking when Johnny picked up the thread of the conversation. "Paul tells me you crated up poor old Vic Barnes and shipped him in. You guys must be crazy. Vic couldn't have had any more to do with this thing then I did; he's not the type. You better let him out. I've got a fishing date with him Thursday."

"Another comedian," Cuneo said disgustedly, and Mike laughed. He had a nice laugh.

"Another? Who? Don't tell me. Let me guess. Johnny. You been on the Ferris wheel with Johnny?"

"That about covers it," Cuneo admitted. "He needs a manager."

"Nobody manages Johnny," Mike Larsen told him.

"No? And what the hell makes him so special?"

"Rogers here knows him; why don't you ask him? I'll give you a hint, though, since you asked me. About a month ago Vic and Johnny and I were fishing out in the Sound. I've got a big old walrus of a thirty-foot overdecked inboard, and I grounded her on a sand bar. I thought for sure we'd have to winch her off, but Johnny jumped out along the bow and got a grip under the water line, and I mean he picked us up and threw us back into Long Island Sound. His shoulders came clear through his shirt, and he was down to his calves in wet sand. You try it some time. I'll take him any day over a truck and give you the odds."

"You his press agent?" Ted Cuneo asked acidly.

"I didn't get a chance to tell you upstairs, Ted," Jimmy Rogers interposed, "but Johnny's the boy who went through the mixmaster overseas with the lieutenant."

"Lieutenant Dameron?" Detective Cuneo's inquiry was sharp. "That character upstairs was part of the lieutenant's show?"

"Make it a little stronger than that."

Hostility bristled in the thin man's tone. "You trying to tell me—"

"They were all specialists, Ted," Detective Rogers said patiently. "Johnny, the lieutenant and Willie Martin, who used to own this hotel here. Johnny and Lieutenant Dameron mutually didn't like each other, but I've heard the lieutenant say himself that, for what they had to, Johnny was only the best. They worked a very tough street, and whenever the steaks fell into the fire Johnny pulled 'em out. The lieutenant was with him when he got those marks on his chest you were asking him about, if you're interested."

"So he's got a few muscles," Ted Cuneo growled irritably. "He still leaves me with an itch. A guy as hairsprung as him—"

"Could get in trouble? The lieutenant maintains that Johnny and trouble are synonymous. Tell you something else —you know that room you just left upstairs? Johnny owns it."

"*Owns* it? This is a hotel, man."

"Regardless, he owns it. Lieutenant Dameron may have

34

felt that Johnny lacked the proper respect for authority, but that bothered Willie Martin not at all. He and Johnny got along fine. Willie brought Johnny back here with him, stuck him in a uniform and let him make a job for himself running the night side. When Willie was in town they shared that room upstairs, otherwise it was Johnny's. A few months back before you came over to this precinct we hit a real twister here and ran up a bag of six bodies in five days. The heat from downtown was enough to fry us, but we were spinning our wheels completely until Johnny aged the lieutenant a few years by strong-arming a solution when he got mad at being pushed around. The kicker turned out to be that the whole circus had been steered here by Willie Martin to darn a hole in his financial sock. By the time Johnny found it out Willie had set a new record for the running broad jump from the twelfth floor. His will left the room and furnishings to Johnny in perpetuity, even if the hotel should be sold. The legal beagles ran in circles for weeks, but it stuck."

Ted Cuneo snorted disgustedly. "He marry anyone in your family? You sound worse than Larsen here."

"You didn't see it happen, Ted. I did. I don't have to like what he does to like the way he does it."

"Ahhhh, the hell with it. Do I genuflect the next time I see him? The hell with it. Let's get to business. Mike, tell me—"

A light came on in a mezzanine office to Johnny's left and distracted him. The shade on the front door came down abruptly, blotting out all but the faintest chinks of light. Public stenographer's office—Johnny looked at his watch. Mighty early for any activity over there. Soft-footedly he eased over toward the chink of light, at the same time trying to keep tuned in on the conversation below him.

"—they did work in the same public relations office?" Cuneo's voice sounded excited. Johnny halted. Who worked?

"That's right." Mike Larsen's voice. "Over a year now."

"Sounds like we should have been talking to you right from the beginning," Cuneo said crisply. "So this Ellen Saxon worked with Barnes' wife? And Barnes goes upstairs for no reason he can give us and finds her body. Very cozy. You think he was doing the tumtiddling bit on his wife?"

"Vic? Vic Barnes? Man, not a chance. Didn't you talk to him?"

"Granted he don't look it; they fool you. Why did he go up there? And why won't he talk about it?"

Mike Larsen's tone was thoughtful. "It's just possible he might think his wife is somehow concerned. Being as how he thinks the sun rises and sets for the sole benefit of Lorraine, if he thought he could save her anything you might have a little trouble with him."

"We're having a little trouble with him." Cuneo's voice was sharp. "I have a hunch you're right. Jimmy, what'd she sound like when you talked to her?"

"Talked to her?" Mike's voice broke in. "When did you talk to her?"

"I went over there." Jimmy Rogers' voice was quiet, but Mike Larsen sounded as if he were having difficulty with his breathing.

"In the middle of the night you went over there? And told her that her husband was in the sneezer for being found in the hotel room of a dead woman who had been her friend? Excuse me. Remind me to cross the street the next time I see you guys coming."

"Don't be such a rose, Mike." Irritation was back in Ted Cuneo's voice. "These people are suspects. You think she was running around on her husband?"

"Now wait a minute. I didn't say that."

"Always the gentleman, eh, Mike?"

"Don't you put words in my mouth, Ted. These people are friends of mine. You go paddle your own canoe. You boys play too rough. I'm through."

"Now wait a minute, Mike—"

Johnny had cautiously resumed his interrupted progress toward the public stenographer's office. He found that even with the shade drawn he could see in through the eight-inch clearance on either side, but what he saw disappointed him. He plainly saw Ed Russo taking a long drink from an up-tilted whisky bottle, and he would much rather have seen Ed Russo doing something—anything at all—which would have permitted Johnny to lower a little weight on him.

Johnny and Ed Russo had hung up a time or two. Verbally. To Johnny's way of thinking, Ed Russo was a man a little bit too impressed with a sense of his own importance. Johnny had often wondered how he and the blonde in the office with him could take a living out of the transient business in a hotel this size, but he conceded that that was their

36

problem. He conceded, too, that it would be difficult to make anything out of Ed Russo taking a drink in his own office, regardless of the hour. He edged back to the front of the balcony.

"—know that Johnny had been married to this girl, Mike?" Detective Rogers sounded quite casual.

"Johnny?" Mike Larsen sounded strangled. "You're crazy!"

"Right from the horse's mouth, Mike. Why should it surprise you so much?"

"Damned if I know, to tell you the truth," Mike admitted after a moment. "Except that I thought I knew Johnny rather well, and I never heard him say a word—"

"The reason I ask is because upstairs he sounded a little bit as though he could be lining up a vendetta for himself. We wouldn't like to see that, Mike. You could do him a favor by warning him off the grass."

Mike snorted. "Joe Dameron could tell you something about warning Johnny off the grass."

"We can't use any help. Or any hindrance. Tell him."

"I'll tell him, and a fat lot of good it will do you."

"Tell him, and let us worry about the good." Footsteps scuffed on the marble floor below; Johnny waited a moment until he was sure they had gone, then descended the stairs into the lobby. Mike Larsen was standing looking thoughtfully out into the foyer after the departed detectives. He turned at the sound of Johnny's approach. "Well . . . speak of the devil—"

"I just heard you speakin' of him." Mike's eyes—cat's eyes, curiously flecked with yellow—went aloft. "Yeah. I was up there. Thanks for the testimonial."

"I'll send you a bill. If you heard it all I can save a little breath."

"You can save a lot of breath."

Mike smiled. "Old head-down Johnny." The smile died. "How come I never heard anything before about you and Ellen?"

"It never seemed to come up."

"Yeah," Mike Larsen said drily. "I can see that. Well, where do we go from here?"

"You think it's too early to call Lorraine? Vic would want one of us to go downtown with her. That Cuneo is all wound up to give her a hard time."

Mike was looking at him curiously. "You think that's a

37

good move? For you to go down there, I mean? You'd be kind of rubbing yourself in Cuneo's nose, wouldn't you? And don't worry about Lorraine; she's no violet. She'll give Cuneo a little better than he's expecting."

"It's Vic I'm thinking of, Mike. He'd expect us to do it."

"Okay," Mike shrugged. "Go ahead and call her; she won't be asleep. I'll pick up a lawyer friend of mine and meet you down there."

Johnny leaned over the registration desk and pulled the front office phone toward himself. "Sally? Ring Vic's place for me, huh?" He twisted the cord in his hand. "Lorraine? Johnny Killain. I'd like to go downtown with you this morning when you go."

"I think I'd like that, Johnny." No hysterics here—a cool, poised voice.

"About nine?"

"I'll be ready."

Mike Larsen nodded as Johnny hung up. "I'll see you down there. And don't you go redheaded on me; I've only got one lawyer friend. And never mind looking at me like the great stone face. Some day I'm going to find something a little thicker than your skull, and when I do the metallurgists are going to beat a path to my door." He stalked out of the lobby, a big man, moving easily.

Johnny resumed his long interrupted trip out back to the kitchen, which was just beginning to stir in the early morning quiet. Two or three lights were on in the big room, and the odor of coffee was in the air. Johnny stopped off by the giant urn and drew off a steaming mug, then carried it over to the paint-peeled desk in the back corner. A round little man with mild blue eyes looked up at his approach. "Good morning, Yonnee."

"Mornin', Eric. What do you feed a kitten?"

The blue eyes considered the matter; the offhand reply was obviously not a part of this man's nature. "Whose kitten, Yonnee?"

"My kitten."

Eric smiled. "I would think then a little liver, a little shrimp, a little milk—"

"You sold me."

Eric rose, his fresh whites rustling. "Drink your coffee. I fix it."

Johnny sipped at the scalding coffee and watched the little

38

second cook unlock a square refrigerator, rummage in its interior and emerge with a slice of liver and a handful of shrimp.

Eric turned to him. "A small kitten, Yonnee?"

Johnny shaped Sassy's size with his hands, and Eric nodded. A wide-bladed knife chopped firmly, and Johnny finished his coffee as wax paper was applied and a pint of milk set out. "Can I have one of those empties, Eric?" Johnny pointed to a stack of cartons which had contained canned goods.

"Why not?"

"Thanks, Eric. For the works." Johnny took a carton whose sides were not too deep, gathered up his packages and departed for the lobby. On the mezzanine he confiscated a medium-sized geranium plant; he uprooted it and dumped the loose dirt in his carton, then slid the empty flower pot with the limp geranium in it under the nearest bench.

In his own room he showed this arrangement to the interested Sassy. "This is light housekeeping, baby doll," he told her, "until Mother Killain gets to do a little shopping." He had already lost her attention; the small, wrinkled nose was testing his packages. "Okay, tiger. Hold tight."

From a shelf above the refrigerator he took down three saucers. He filled one with milk and put a little shrimp and a little liver in each of the others. As an afterthought he placed a newspaper beneath them, and Sassy immediately made it look like an excellent idea. Her notion of a quiet meal was to charge up on a plate full tilt and seize a piece in her mouth, then back away growling, defying the world to take it away from her. At the extreme edge of the newspaper she would eat daintily, then crouch and rush back again. She was an extremely leisurely diner.

He watched her for a few moments, then filled another saucer with water and added it to the lineup. He stretched out on the bed and closed his eyes lightly; in the first peaceful interlude he had had since Vic Barnes had opened Ellen Saxon's door Johnny tried to filter through his mind the impossible sequence of events since two o'clock that morning. For a long time the only noises in the room were Sassy's small sounds and the spatter of her paws on the newspaper.

CHAPTER 5

Johnny pushed the little stack of transcript sheets, telephone chits and miscellaneous charges across the registration desk to Marty Seiden, a dapper, thin-faced youngster with a ready smile who worked as one of the day front-desk men. "This is a dirty trick, kid," Johnny began; he nodded apologetically at the stack of paperwork. "You think you can straighten it out? Vic hadn't made much of a dent in it before they put the snatch on him. Paul posted the telephone charges, but that's about all that's been done."

"A cinch, big man," Marty said confidently. His oversized bow tie matched his flaming red hair; he was already rolling back his cuffs. "Don't worry about it. Did you balance his cash?"

"Me? I couldn't balance my pocket change." Johnny pushed a key over the counter. "I locked it up. And listen, Marty. When a guy works a cash drawer, sometimes he floats a little paper against pay day. You know?"

"I know." The redhead grinned. "If I need anything to make it right before I send it upstairs I'll let you know." He lined up three long yellow pencils beside the sharpener before he looked over at Johnny again. "If Vic's going to be under glass on this awhile, you're going to need a pencil man nights. How about me?"

Johnny nodded. "You just graduated to sleepin' days, kid. I'll square it with Rollins right now. See you tonight." He crossed the lobby and mounted to the executive offices on the mezzanine. Inside the first door was a double row of frosted-glass partitioned cubicles; he knocked upon the door marked AUDITOR, and nodded to the heavy-featured man in the horn-rimmed glasses behind the cluttered desk as he entered. "Mornin', Chet. You got any objections to lettin' Marty Seiden work the night side with me till we spring Vic?"

Bushy brows behind the glasses climbed expressively.

40

"Marty? Might not be a bad idea. He's a good man with figures; he'll keep you afloat. He's a little flip with his tongue; don't hesitate to sandpaper him down if he gets out of line. Do him good."

"How's Arthur J. Morrison going to take all this, Chet?"

The auditor leaned back in his chair and light glinted from his glasses. "Officially, he's going to be a little sticky. The night front-desk man up in a guest's room at three in the morning, the guest a woman, and deceased; you understand the manager's attitude has to be a little professional. Unoffically, he's already called me to ask if I thought there was anything he could do."

"Yeah? Not bad. We'll worry about his official attitude when we get Vic unstuck downtown. You'll transfer Marty over?"

"Right now."

"Thanks, Chet." Johnny walked back out to the mezzanine from the office. He stopped on the landing; Mike Larsen was in the middle of the stairs on his way up, and he was coming three steps at a time. He pulled up in front of Johnny, breathing hard, and shoved a newspaper at him.

"Look at this!"

Johnny caught the blare of a headline in the paper pushed at him. "You mean we made the front page?"

"No, no." Mike pointed. "Not here. Read it."

Johnny looked at the black, block print. ROBERT SANDERS KILLED AT APARTMENT DOOR. And in the subheading in smaller print, *Prominent Public Relations Expert and Clubman Shot Four Times*. The story started, "Robert Sanders, 54, 219 Cypress Lane, was shot and killed by as yet unknown assailants in the driveway of the co-operative apartment where he made his home. The body was discovered—"

Mike Larsen's voice was tense as Johnny lowered the paper and looked at him inquiringly. "Robert Sanders owned the business where Ellen and Lorraine worked."

Johnny flattened the paper for another look. "When—"

"Sometime after midnight, it says. Body found at three-forty-five A.M. by a neighbor."

Johnny stared at the subheading. "Four times—"

"What?"

"Nothing." Here was a guy in a groove—four shots for Sanders, and four shots from the dark sedan. "This kind of starches things, Mike. Looks like we only had the semi-windup here; the main event was across town. You can bet me it was under the same auspices."

"How do you figure that?"

"The batting order's got to be Sanders first, then Ellen. Ellen was over there, and if she didn't actually see it she saw or sensed enough to scare her green. Trouble was the pistol-packin' type saw Ellen, too, and followed her over here. Followed her right inside after I slowed him up on the street. A strong move. No Pollyanna, this citizen."

"What's this about a slow-up on the street?"

Johnny explained. "The police should tie this into a pretty tight knot, Mike; the guy dug a furrow all the way across town."

Mike looked doubtful; the yellow-flecked eyes returned to the paper. "Even supposing the time element is right, Johnny, it would still be a pretty good trick—"

"Even better than you know." Johnny thought of the unregistered room, and shook his head. "The thing I want to know is how a guy like that could get upstairs in the place here without being seen by Vic or Paul or me. Strangers get asked questions, but nobody blew a whistle." He looked at Mike. "What kind of a guy was this Sanders?"

"I guess I'd have to say he was a good businessman—"

"Public-relationese for a hard-nosed bulldozer?"

Mike waved a hand as he seated himself on a leather-covered bench. "Speak no evil. He was smooth, and he got along. His wife was his partner in the business, and she was every bit as good as he was. I've heard rumors it wasn't much of a marriage, but nobody could say that about the business tie-up. They were good."

"Was Ellen running around with this Sanders?"

"No." Mike tasted the word, leaned back and tried it again, less positively. "No. I never saw them together, and I never heard anyone say they'd seen them together—"

"But there was something?"

"All right." Mike stood up abruptly. "I'd heard . . . stories." His hand gesture was impatient. "You can always hear stories. Once in a while they might even be true."

"You told Ted Cuneo that Lorraine Barnes wasn't running around with Sanders. That on the level?"

As suddenly as he had stood up, Mike Larsen sat down. "What made you ask that?" He spread his hands. "We live in an imperfect world, Johnny."

42

"Yeah. And now we got a self-appointed critic runnin' around and leveling off imperfections. No reservations on this Lorraine Barnes-Robert Sanders *ménage-a-deux?*"

"No reservations. Which isn't to say that there are any notarized affidavits on file—" He hesitated and ran a hand over his chin. "This stuff I just told you—"

"I'm takin' a page in the *Times*. You get the by-line."

Mike's grin was sheepish. "All right, I shouldn't have said it. You going by for Lorraine?"

"Yeah. What's she like, really? I don't think I've even seen her more than three or four times, when I'd stop by to pick up Vic when we were going fishin'."

This time Mike's grin was cynical. "How do the poets put it? Fire-and-ice. For once you're well matched. She can melt down a bronze idol with her tongue, and she's right in your class in rocketry take-off. She has a very definite mind of her own. Keep your left hand high."

Johnny grunted, waved idly and turned to the stairs. He walked the short distance to Vic's place; it was only six blocks east and two south of the hotel, one of the occasional half-block enclaves of apartments in midtown New York's business jungle. He walked because he needed to think, and he felt that he had the germ of something that needed thinking about.

He knew now why Vic had gone up to Ellen Saxon's room. Check that, Killain—by a process of elimination you think you know. Only one thing in the world could have taken him up there.

Somehow Lorraine Barnes had known that Ellen Saxon was in the hotel, and Lorraine had called Vic. To give Ellen a message or to bring her to the phone, more likely. Wait a minute—how did Vic know where she was? He didn't even know she was there at all until Lorraine told him so.

Johnny worried it around, unconsciously walking faster. Vic had to know, somehow; it was the only thing that made sense. And because Ellen was in an unregistered room it would have complicated things for Vic to call her through the hotel switchboard. He had to go up there to deliver the message, whatever it was. And finding the body and not knowing how deeply Lorraine was involved, Vic had gone into the deep freeze rather than say the wrong thing.

How had Lorraine known Ellen was in the hotel? There was only one way that she could have known. She had to

43

have been someplace close to whatever it was that had panicked Ellen. If it hadn't been Lorraine herself, Johnny reminded himself suddenly. He tried again to think of the figure hunched down over the steering wheel of the dark sedan. Could it have been a woman? He shook his head; he didn't know. Could Lorraine have killed Robert Sanders and followed Ellen Saxon back to the hotel to kill her, too? Possible. Not probable. For one thing, Lorraine was known to hotel personnel. Still—

He looked up and around suddenly. His preoccupation had carried him half a block beyond Vic's apartment, and he turned and retraced his steps. Seen in the daylight, the neighborhood and the building were depressing. A rust-streaked iron fence with blunted pikes stood sentinel across the building's frontage and on both sides of the walk to the front door. He entered the gate and strode up the narrow cement strip; once past the door the vestibule was more spacious and attractive than hinted. at by the exterior.

He pressed the button beneath the neatly lettered name plate, and tried to visualize Lorraine Barnes from the few times he had met her. A no-nonsense woman, he would have summarized it. Younger than Vic. No beauty. Attractive? He tried to remember; somehow—

The buzzer blasted through his reverie, and he leaned into the mouthpiece. "Johnny."

"Come right up."

He knew it was the second floor; he walked up, and she was standing in the open door of the apartment when he emerged into the hall from the landing. She stood aside to let him enter. "I do appreciate your taking this trouble, Johnny."

He listened to the cool voice; he waited while she closed the door, then followed her inside from the short hall into a living room furnished in quiet good taste. A sofa of the type that could be made into a bed ran along the longest wall, and two comfortable armchairs were at the far end of the room facing the television set. The sofa's and armchairs' slipcovers were a flowered pastel, and almost matched the drapes. A wedding picture stood beside the percolator on the coffee table, and Johnny looked down at a younger-looking Vic and a Lorraine who seemed not to have changed at all.

"Coffee?" she asked him. "It's all ready. Sit down."

He didn't want the coffee, but he wanted to talk. He sat

44

down. He watched her brisk movements; he knew now that he had forgotten the details of her looks in the intervals between seeing her. And she *was* attractive. About thirty-five. Good figure. Very good. Hair well kept up. A detached attitude, and an expression to match.

He looked at the high neckline on her light blue sleeveless dress with its ruffled collar. Go ahead, Killain; ask her if she's scratched up under that high neckline. Sure, go ahead and ask her. This is only Vic's wife.

She served him on a small tray, bringing it over to his chair, black coffee with a tiny matched creamer and sugar bowl. As he sweetened the coffee she nodded to something back of him, and he half turned to look at the small bag on the floor. "I packed a few things for Vic I thought he might like to have." Johnny nodded, and she continued evenly, with no particular emphasis in her tone. "Since I heard the radio this morning I'm not so sure I shouldn't pack one for myself."

Johnny didn't pretend to misunderstand. "This Sanders thing? The police call you?"

"Not this morning." Her lips smiled, but her eyes didn't. "I imagine they'll feel confident of getting it all at this session to which they so politely invited me. I'm afraid the whole thing could be a bit of a mess."

He looked at her curiously. "In what way?"

"There are . . . ramifications. Ellen ran a bookkeeping machine over at the office. I'd been a stenographer until recently. Ellen—"

"Until recently?"

The light-colored eyes—gray? Blue-gray, Johnny decided —never wavered. "I've been acting as private secretary to Mr. Sanders." Johnny held his tongue as her pause seemed to invite comment. When she resumed she had changed direction. "Did Ellen come directly to you last night? Or this morning, rather?"

"Yeah." He sat up alertly. "Why?"

"Because I sent her to you." Lorraine Barnes smiled faintly. "A fact I believe you would have deduced eventually. She refused to come back here with me, and she was afraid to go home. I finally suggested you. She jumped at it."

"A lot of good I did her." His voice was harsh. "Where was this?"

45

She turned a hand over palm down, resignedly. "Let's say in the very near vicinity of Robert Sanders' apartment."

"Did you know Sanders was dead?"

"No. I might have managed differently if I had, but that's hindsight, of course. I only knew that Ellen had seen something that had frightened her nearly out of her mind. I couldn't get a coherent sentence out of her. We couldn't stand on the sidewalk; I put her in a cab and sent her on to you."

"Do you know why Ellen was there, or with whom?"

"No. She would answer no questions at all. I came back here, but I couldn't leave it alone. I had to know what had frightened her, or I felt that I did. I had something at stake myself. I called Vic at the hotel and asked him to have her call me back. He was surprised; asked me why I thought she'd be there. I told him I'd sent her to you, and he said oh, yes, that he knew where she was, but why on earth he went up there—"

"He got a bad break on that." Johnny explained about the unregistered room. "With Ellen not registered, there was no rack or phone listing for her. Vic could have asked the operator to ring an unregistered room, but since it was me that put Ellen in there he might have thought it was important to me not to have the operator know it. When he found the body he didn't know if or how deeply you were involved, so he said nothing."

This time it was Lorraine Barnes' turn to say nothing in a pause that invited comment. While the silence lengthened she studied a fingernail's gloss and buffed it lightly on a fold of her dress. She spoke finally as Johnny was casting about in his mind for a fresh assault upon her glacial calm. "I'm not going to tell the police that I was anywhere near Robert Sanders' apartment this morning, Johnny."

He stared at her. "That's your business, but you know they're gonna shake you to your back teeth? You think you can make it stick?"

"I'm relieved to hear you say that it's my business. As for making it stick—why, you never know until you try." Her voice was quiet, unruffled. Nerve, he thought admiringly. She had nerve in great, jumped-up bunches. "I believe that Ellen was the only one who saw me; I'm going to hope that she was." Her tone was factual, with no hint of apology. "You see, Johnny, for Vic there can be no satisfactory explanation

46

for my being in that neighborhood this morning. I wish no further involvement. Vic would want it that way."

The hell of it is, Johnny thought, Vic *would* want it that way. This cool-voiced little witch might be the whore of all the world, but Vic would want what she wanted. He put down his coffee cup. "If you're not going to tell the police why did you tell me?"

She smiled, the same faint smile that was not really a smile at all. "A calculated risk. You're no fool, Johnny. Sooner or later you would have figured out what sent Vic up to Ellen's room. If you were going to tell the police everything you know, or suspect, there wasn't a great deal of point in what I was planning. I had to know where I stood."

"What makes you think I haven't told them everything, or won't this morning? I'm under the gun downtown, too, you know."

She considered him steadily. "I don't have to be right, but I think you're a little too primitive for that." She removed a pair of white gloves from her handbag. "Are we ready?"

"You may think you know what you're doing," Johnny pointed out as he rose to his feet, "but on the street where I live you'd be classified in a hurry. Fruitcake. Grade A."

"If there's a medal goes with it I may apply later."

"You could be forgetting one important item," he suggested. "For my money, somebody killed Sanders, then followed Ellen across town and killed her. You were with Ellen, for a few minutes anyway. If the killer saw you too, where does that leave you?"

Lorraine Barnes drew on her gloves with a snap. "Next in line, you mean? I would very much like to see him try to kill me."

Could that be because you know who he is? Johnny thought to himself. And have your own reasons for not naming him? Or because you're the killer and so have nothing to fear?

He stepped forward silently and picked up Vic's bag. Anyone who could follow the twists and turns in this woman could solve a couple of murders in his spare time. He followed Lorraine Barnes to the door.

The searing midday heat on the street drove Johnny along the steaming sidewalk on his way back to the hotel. The combination of no sleep, summer sun and a grueling three-hour session downtown had left him frayed. He would welcome the air-conditioned lobby.

He had lost his temper, of course. He always did. They had come at him in relays, pulling and hauling, reworking the same tired ground. In the final hour he had taken himself to his surest refuge—animal silence. They had tired of it, finally, and turned him out after he had signed his formal statement.

Lorraine Barnes was still being questioned, but Johnny felt few qualms about her. There was a woman for you. She had politely but firmly chased the lawyer Mike Larsen had sent —Mike had inexplicably not shown—and Johnny had waited beside her phone booth while she called her own lawyer and calmly instructed him that if he had not heard from her by three o'clock that he was to do whatever was necessary to release her.

He shook his head as he turned into the hotel foyer from the sizzling sidewalk. On the record today, Lorraine Barnes had more backbone and know-how than the average National Guard unit. Women—try to figure them, and lose your mind.

He could see Gus Poulles through the glass doors which separated the foyer from the lobby. Gus was Johnny's counterpart on the morning shift, the day bell captain, a pale, blackhaired Greek with sunken, worldly eyes. Johnny emerged into the lobby's chill breath and walked to the desk; he and Gus had little need for extended conversation. They understood each other. Gus was a realist; he drifted through the hotel day after day fatalistically absorbing man's frailties.

The dark eyes inspected Johnny. "Bad?"

"Not good. They're still holding him." Johnny frowned. "They act a little frantic down there. I don't get it. It can't be all that complicated, not when you can lean all over people the way they can. They seem—"

Gus held up a hand as his phone rang. "Bell captain, good morning." He listened and looked at Johnny sardonically as the fingers of his free hand delicately pinched his nostrils. "No, sir. Not since I've been on." He bowed to the phone, the mobile features twisted into a caricature of a sweet smile. "I'll check, Mr. Russo." He covered the mouthpiece and called over his shoulder to the checkroom behind him. "Angelo! Anyone leave a white kitten here for Russo this morning?"

The short hairs on the back of Johnny's neck lifted; how many white kittens figured to be around this place?

"—sorry," Gus was saying. "If it comes in I'll call you."

"Russo," Johnny said thoughtfully as Gus hung up. "Ed Russo. Edmund Russo, Esquire. Public stenographer's office on the mezzanine. A wheel. A big, round wheel. He wanted information from me about a guest once; surprised as hell when he didn't get it. A roughrider. Wears his spurs twenty-four hours a day."

Gus nodded, dark eyes amused. "Chapter and verse."

"Yeah." Johnny straightened. "A self-appointed hard guy. And now he's interested in white kittens? Somehow I don't think he's the type. Not the type at all. I think I'll go see."

"Hey—" Gus's voice trailed off behind Johnny, already moving in the direction of the stairs. Russo's query could be a coincidence, and again it might not. Johnny climbed the stairs; in motion he felt loose and easy, freed from the burden of doubt and self-blame he had felt since the first moment he had seen Ellen's body.

The shade on the door of the public stenographer's office was still drawn securely, as it had been earlier that morning. Johnny didn't bother to knock when the doorknob responded to his inquiring rotation; the tiny outer office was dark as he entered. The chair usually occupied by the vividly blonde Miss Mavis Delaroche had been pushed neatly beneath her kneehole desk. A voice cleared itself and addressed Johnny raggedly from the interior. "Sorry. We're closed."

Johnny walked over to the door which led to the larger back office; Ed Russo sat behind his own desk, the top of which was furnished solely with a bottle and glass, each half empty. He looked up impatiently as Johnny's shadow fell across his desk. "Sorry." He took another look and obviously disapproved of what he saw. "Oh. Outside, Killain. I'm busy."

"You look busy." Johnny estimated him; Edmund Russo was a slim, usually polished individual right now in need of a little refurbishing. The narrow face needed a shave, the suit was rumpled, the tie loosened, the collar wilted, the eyes bloodshot.

Russo half rose in his chair at Johnny's steady regard. "Get out of here, will you? We're closed. Come on—blow."

Johnny sat down leisurely in a chair opposite him, and Russo's knuckles whitened as he leaned forward over his desk. "You hear me?" he demanded hoarsely. "Get out!"

49

"This a public stenographer's office?" Johnny inquired mildly. "I want to send a letter."

"You never sent a letter in your damn life. I already told you we're closed. Do you see Mavis out there? Now rack it up and drag."

Johnny settled more solidly in his chair. "This letter is about a white kitten."

Russo stared; he sat down slowly. "What do you know about—" He chopped off whatever he had been about to say and reached blindly for his glass. He swallowed lengthily and wiped his lips with the back of his hand. He glared at Johnny, and his voice was stronger. "Beat it. Right now. Or I call the manager's office, wise guy."

"Let's take it a little slower, Russo." Johnny's voice hardened. "When I roomed Ellen Saxon last night she had a white kitten for you. Did you go upstairs to get it?"

The slim man slumped in his chair; the bloodshot eyes stared at Johnny. Then he seemed to re-cock himself joint by joint as reaction came to him. "Wise guy!" he sputtered again as he surged erect; his hand closed on the neck of the whisky bottle, and in one blurred, sweeping movement he fired it at Johnny's head. Johnny's instinctive move to the side got his head out of line, but not his shoulder; the bottle hit him heavily, bounced off and smashed on the parqueted floor.

Ed Russo had continued on around his desk in a stumbling run; Johnny was still only two-thirds of the way upright after the impact of the bottle when the flailing hands were pounding at his face. For an instant he absorbed the tattoo, then impatiently locked his hands together under Russo's chest and shoved. The man staggered back, and Johnny straightened up and moved away from the chair that hampered him. When Russo regained his balance and charged again, head down, Johnny sighted down the angle and put his shoulder behind the hard right-hand smash that caught the incoming jawline and blasted it floorward in a careening arc. Ed Russo slid on past into the corner and stayed there, and Johnny experimentally fingered a tingling spot on his own cheekbone.

He flexed his right hand and looked down at Russo and at the puddle of whisky and glass fragments on the floor. "Quite a reaction," Johnny told the unconscious man aloud.

50

"I'd have to say you act like a man with something on his mind."

He walked around behind Russo's desk and, after considering a moment, jerked open the center drawer. He didn't know what he expected to find, but he blinked down at the newspaper folded to the black headline proclaiming the death of Robert Sanders.

He stood, looked at the far wall and silently slid the drawer shut. Robert Sanders. Ellen Saxon. Edmund Russo. Now what kind of a round robin was that? He groped around in his mind for a hook, a possible connection. He sighed, finally; he needed to do some thinking.

He left the office without a backward glance.

CHAPTER 6

WALTER STEWART STRAIGHTENED IN HIS SWIVEL CHAIR at the sound of the tap-tap of high heels approaching the partly opened door of his office; his blunt-fingered, capable-looking hands rapidly shuffled the cardboard folders on his desk. He was a slender man in an untidy-looking, expensively cut dark suit; he had a lean, aggressive face, and his graying hair thinned out on top to a noticeable bald spot. He glanced up at the open door with studied casualness as Florence Richardson entered.

"You're staying on this evening, Mr. Stewart?"

Her voice was low-keyed—like her personality, he thought. And her appearance. Attractive enough, with the fresh, clear complexion contrasted with the prematurely gray hair, but the severely tailored suit and the glasses militated against the masculine head-turn in a crowd, the hallmark of the man's woman.

"A few moments only, Miss Richardson." He nodded down at the opened folders in front of him. "I have a late dinner engagement, and I thought I might use the time profitably to update one or two of these programs."

"If there's anything I can do—"

51

"Nothing, thanks. I'm just noodling, actually."

"Well, if you're sure . . . you'll get the safe?"

"I won't forget. I'll take care of it."

"I'll put the night latch on the outer door as I leave. Good night, Mr. Stewart."

"Good night, Miss Richardson." He sat and listened again to the tap-tap of her heels, diminishing now, and then the slight sound of the door. Capable girl—damn capable. He was lucky to have her. Kept the office running like a watch, and no fuss and feathers about it, either.

He pushed a folder absently along the side of his desk with a stiffened forefinger and leaned back lazily in his chair and folded his hands behind his head. He stared for a moment at the far wall with its framed certificates, an idle toe tapping idly on the inner well of the desk. He unclasped his hands and stood up restlessly, shoving the hands deeply into his pockets.

He wandered out into the outer office, from whose floor space his own partitioned-off, glassed-in privacy had been carved. It was quiet now in the office after the daylong tac-tac-tac of the machines. Approvingly he noted the neat, clean desk tops; he insisted upon a clean desk at quitting time. A six-girl office, Stewart, he reminded himself; do you remember when you used to wonder if you'd ever have a one-girl office? Or a place of your own at all? And not so long ago, either.

He glanced at the gold lettering on the heavily frosted glass of the outer door; it always reassured him to see it there. He was reading it backward from where he stood, of course, but then he really didn't need to read it at all. He'd carried those letters of gold in his heart for ten years before he ever got them up on glass. *Walter Stewart, Insurance Broker.* And directly beneath in smaller block print, WE SELL SERVICE. Neat, but not gaudy. Conservative insurance service for conservative clients. Too bad you couldn't put that up on the door, too.

He rested an elbow on a chest-high, olive green filing cabinet, and as an afterthought tested the top drawer. Locked, as it should be. Miss Richardson checked them personally each evening before she left; he'd never found her to be careless. Away from the office as much as he was, it was a relief not to have to be eternally concerned with the grinding function of the hour-by-hour small emergencies of office routine. Miss

Richardson handled it all. He himself had no patience for such details; he begrudged the time spent in such fashion as a distraction from a broker's true *métier*. He—

Three sharp raps on the glass aroused him; he crossed to the gold-lettered door, opened it and stood aside. "Come in."

A big man entered; he was dressed flamboyantly in a vividly checked sport coat and light-colored slacks. He wore an expensive panama with a too-wide brim, and he had a livid scar that slightly pulled down a corner of the heavy mouth. The face was a scarred full moon.

Walter Stewart led the way directly back to the inner office, and pulled the guest chair up beside his desk. The big man seated himself and removed a small notebook from an inside breast pocket which he passed across the desk to Walter Stewart, who thumbed casually through its closely written contents, then nodded. He opened the center drawer of his desk and took out a sealed white envelope; he leaned forward slightly to hand it to the big man, who slit the flap with a thumbnail, removed the small sheaf of bills, flipped them between thumb and forefinger as casually as Walter Stewart had thumbed the notebook, restored the bills to the envelope and the envelope to the inside breast pocket.

Not a word had been spoken during the almost ritualistic transfer, but as the big man made a movement to rise Walter Stewart raised a hand.

"One moment," he said. His eyes followed the movement of his hands on the desk top as they faced two folders together on the blotter. He kept his eyes on the folders as he continued. "I find that I shan't need the service any longer." He forced himself to look across the desk.

"Sorry to hear it, Mr. Stewart." There was no change of expression on the heavy features; in the quiet office the voice was a rolling bass, ruggedly deep. "We're a little bit proud of our service. Is it something specific?"

"Not at all," Walter Stewart said. He said it hastily. "It's the fact rather that circumstances have changed—" He paused; he didn't like the sound of the phrase. He tried again. "There eventually comes a time when it becomes necessary to reassess a given situation."

"In other words, you feel you've outgrown us, Mr. Stewart."

Walter Stewart restrained the impulsive reply on the tip of his tongue. He felt warmth invading his features, but he made himself speak calmly. "Such a statement implies ingrati-

53

tude on my part. I neither feel nor wish to be made to feel ungrateful."

"Look at it from our point of view." The heavy voice rolled over Walter Stewart as the big man leaned back in his chair and ran his eye appraisingly from the comfortably furnished office in which they sat on out to the spacious exterior. "I've been making these little visits to you for about four years now, Mr. Stewart. Not always to this address; three different addresses, I believe. Each in turn a little more substantial, a little more fashionable. You've prospered; you've moved on and up. Do you remember the first address, Mr. Stewart?"

Walter Stewart did remember; he sat, silent. The big man waved a negligent hand about him. "I personally much prefer this address, and the circumstances it represents. I think you do, too. My associates and I like to feel that our service was of some material help to you in attaining the address and circumstances. You know the expense involved in maintaining our service; it is an expense which we can support only by a firm, equitable arrangement with our clients. You follow me, Mr. Stewart?"

Walter Stewart circled dry lips with his tongue. "I have always felt our arrangement to be equitable."

"Exactly," the heavy voice said, and waited.

Walter Stewart sought for words. He was clever with words, but he could find none at the moment to avoid the direct question he had previously side-stepped. Despite himself his voice sharpened. "Do you take the attitude then that this arrangement is permanent?"

"A matter of terminology. I myself prefer the word 'Irrevocable'."

"I refuse to concede——" Walter Stewart broke off suddenly. His blunt fingers drummed rapidly on the desk top. He looked up in sudden alarm as the big man rose, but there was a smile on the moon face. Or it could have been a smile except for the scar.

"You'll excuse me, I'm sure, Mr. Stewart. I have another appointment. I'd like to leave you with this thought. My associates and I dislike sounding arbitrary, but we feel that over the years our relationship has developed into something mutually profitable. We wouldn't like to see the status quo disturbed. We really wouldn't, believe me." Thick fingers flirted with the too-wide brim of the panama as he settled

54

it more firmly on his head. "See you next month, Mr. Stewart. As usual. Unless you call. And if I were you, I wouldn't call. Good night."

Walter Stewart sat and listened to the tread of the heavy footsteps, cut off by the sound of the closing door. He drew a long breath, and stared down unseeingly at the blotter on his desk.

So now you know, Stewart. Now you know.

He sank back in his chair and closed his eyes, then leaned forward as he forced himself to open them again. What are you worried about? he asked himself impatiently. Nothing has changed. Not one single thing has changed.

Blackmail. He rolled it around on his tongue. He shrugged; sticks and stones may break your bones, Stewart, but names will never hurt you. You may be tied to the railroad track, but as the man very carefully pointed out you like the way you're living, too.

There's no difference, except that now you know that you bought the whirlwind.

And haven't you really always known?

Johnny sat bolt upright on the bed, startled from sleep by a thumping on his chest. His instinctively quick movement dislodged the scampering Sassy, who bounded down to the end of the bed and turned to wrinkle her nose at him disapprovingly. "You got to cut that out, baby doll; I might swing first and look later."

He stretched and looked at the late afternoon sunlight beneath the three-quarters-drawn shade. Might as well get up and eat. He lay back and stared up at the ceiling. He'd get going in a minute; shower first, shave . . .

Sassy boarded his right leg, walked smoothly up the length of his body, and resettled herself on his chest, face-to-face. He looked down at the blue eyes and the serious little face. "You've sure taken over this quarter-deck, white stuff. Something tells me I've gone under new management."

The kitten's eyes were tightly closed as she licked diligently at a paw; Johnny snapped his fingers at her, but she paid no attention. When she was satisfied with the condition of the paw she lifted her head and looked at him again. This time when he snapped she grabbed for the fingers. Mildly curious, he extended his arm behind the small head and

55

snapped the fingers again. She was watching his face and made no movement.

Johnny began to get a feeling. "You little sinner, you're deaf." He sat up halfway, holding her on his chest, experimenting. When she could see the snapping fingers Sassy went for them. When she couldn't there was no reaction.

He lifted her free from his chest at the expense of some skin as her claws hooked in instinctively. He swung his legs over the edge of the bed and put the kitten on the floor between his feet, faced away from him; the first four or five times he removed his hand from the small body she turned immediately to see what new game they were playing. He waited patiently until she wearied of turning and lay quietly with only the switching tail in motion. When he was sure she couldn't see him he picked up a shoe and let it fall heavily, and Sassy bounded up and switched ends in mid-air, coming down facing him.

"You just kiddin' around with me, sugarpuss? You heard that, all right. Or wait a minute. Do you hear it or do you get the vibration from the floor in your paws?"

He faced her about again, and when she was quiet clapped his hands together with a report that surprised even himself. The kitten never even quivered. He lifted a foot and jammed his bare heel down hard, and although the noise was only a light thud Sassy again performed her switched-ends ballet.

No doubt about it—the kitten was deaf. She was extremely sensitive to all vibrations—and even to air currents, he could see now that he was watching her closely. The small, questing nose was rarely still, and a breeze barely light enough to flutter a curtain's gauze at the window was sufficient to bring her head around inquiringly.

He reached down and picked her up again and put her back on his chest as he stretched out. "All right, baby doll. It's tough, but if you never had it you don't miss it. And nature's law of compensation seems to have you doing all right for yourself."

Sassy reached a tentative paw toward his moving lips, and he took the paw in his hand. Immediately the tufted ears flattened; she half rolled on her side in an attempt to get at the holding hand with her other paw. He swept her off his chest down onto her back on the bed beside him and tickled the furry underbelly, and for an instant all four legs

56

furiously resented this indignity before she stretched languidly and invited more.

Johnny laughed, played with her for another moment and then stuffed her under the sheet as he slid off the bed. He stood and watched her battle her way out, to emerge with fangs bared, ears cocked and tail thrashing. She glared about the bed for him, then in a kittenishly instantaneous change of mood collapsed flexibly upon herself as she energetically cleaned a hind leg.

Johnny picked up her saucers from the newspaper on the floor and rinsed them clean. He refilled them from the wax-papered cache and the milk carton in the refrigerator. The instant he stooped over the newspaper, saucers in hand, a white streak leaped from the bed and trotted over to him, white paws twinkling and tail aloft like a Saracen banner.

He went into the bathroom and turned on the shower; he stood in a torrent of hot water and then of cold, and dashed out puffing and blowing. Halfway through his shave he remembered something and in his underwear went to the phone and gave the operator the number of Vic's apartment. "Lorraine? Johnny. Since you're home I don't know that I even need to ask, but how'd you make out with the boys?"

He caught her hesitation. "Where are you calling from, Johnny?"

"The hotel."

"Do you think that's wise? Have you eaten yet?"

"Just on my way downstairs."

"Why don't you come over and eat with me? It's too hot to fuss, but if a salad will tempt you—"

It was his turn to hesitate, but only for an instant. "Be there in thirty minutes."

"Fine. I'll be expecting you."

He stared down at the phone musingly as he replaced it. Just where did he stand with this woman? She was the wife of a good friend. By her own admission she wasn't a perfect wife. She had been tied up with Robert Sanders, professionally and—according to Mike Larsen—otherwise. She could have killed Robert Sanders. And whoever had killed Robert Sanders had more than likely killed Ellen Saxon. Johnny frowned down at his clenched hands; tonight he would clear out a little underbrush. The machete would probably draw a little blood, but so be it.

57

He finished shaving, whacked at his still damp hair a couple of times with the comb, dressed quickly, waved to the preoccupied Sassy and left the room. On the street the heat rose up and attacked him. He whistled for a cab; in the back seat the little breeze that they stirred up was a hot breeze. The city lay limp in the kiln.

Lorraine Barnes had the apartment door ajar when he came off the second floor landing; he knocked on the partly opened door.

"Come in," she said from just inside.

He went in through the hall to the living room, where she was setting up collapsible little tables. "You look to see who you were inviting in?" he asked her, indicating the still open door in the hall.

"No." She straightened, thoughtful. "I never even thought about it, since I knew you were coming—"

"I'd start thinking about it. There's no inoculation—"

"Sit down," she interrupted firmly. "Food first, lectures later." Johnny sat down, and she placed on the little table before him a platter piled high with potato salad, pineapple slices, hard-boiled eggs, lettuce, tomatoes, radishes, cucumbers, cold cuts and cheese. He blinked up at her.

"Half of this is enough for the Mexican Army."

"Eat." A smaller tray with a tall glass, a pitcher of ice and a pitcher of tea was added to his table. "Speak up for what you don't see."

For a short time the clink of cutlery and the tinkle of ice was the only sound in the room. When Johnny sank back with a repleted sigh Lorraine removed his tray. She had already removed her own. She lit two cigarettes and offered him one, and as he inhaled she sat down across from him again.

"I think I owe you an explanation, Johnny." He had intended to give her no opportunity to speak first, but he realized that he had been outmaneuvered. The blue-gray eyes across the room were fixed upon him steadily. "Cards face up? All the way around?"

He nodded, warily.

She crossed her legs deliberately and tugged her skirt down over her knees. "I had a choice when I went down there this morning. I could tell them where I'd been last night, and in fact and inference explain Vic's presence in Ellen's room. I think they'd let him go if I did—soon, any-

58

way. I didn't tell them, and I suppose you think I'm a first-class heel."

He dragged hard on the cigarette. "It's your problem." He couldn't keep the irritation from his voice.

"Granted. I'll handle it. Myself." Twilight had stolen up to the apartment windows; he sat and watched the cigarette in the chair opposite glow more brightly as Lorraine Barnes continued. "There is a husband-and-wife relationship almost impossible to describe to an outsider. You're Vic's friend, so I'm trying. I'm also trying because I'd like your help." The cigarette in her hand moved in a vague arc; the steady voice was expressionless. "Vic is not a passionate man. It has nothing to do with his age; he never has been. In our marriage there are really only two things I can give him: companionship, and his own self-respect. I've compromised the self-respect, but I don't intend for Vic to know it. Vic needs me, depends upon me; I'm his crutch against the world. And in turn I'm very grateful to him for being the sweet person that he is." Above the smoldering cigarette her gaze was unwinking. "I wouldn't want you to think this an excuse or a rationalization, even. I'm simply trying to explain to you the position in which I find myself."

He stirred uneasily in his chair. "So where does it leave you?"

"That depends on you. Do you think I killed Ellen, Johnny?"

He drew in his breath; this woman beat him to first one punch and then another. For the space of ten seconds he turned it over in his mind, and then he spoke deliberately. "I don't know. I doubt that a woman would have the strength; Ellen was no midget. On the other hand, you had opportunity as far as Sanders and Ellen both were concerned, so far as I know, and I have to think that whoever got Sanders got Ellen, too." He was silent a moment. "I don't know about Sanders, but there's one way you can get yourself ninety-five per cent clean with me on Ellen. The police didn't put it out, but Ellen reached whoever killed her with her fingernails—reached them good. This morning when we went downtown you had on a high-necked dress. You've got another on now. I want a look. To the waist."

She said nothing at all for a count of twenty, and when she did speak her voice was an octave lower. "If I didn't need you—" She said it between her teeth as she stood up.

"I'm in this thing, and I want out with as whole a skin as I can manage. Sit where you are." She unfastened the three small mother-of-pearl buttons at the neck of her dress and in one long flowing motion stooped, caught up the hem of her skirt and pulled the dress off over her head. She had on a half-slip and a bra. In seconds she had the bra unhooked and off, and made one slow, complete pirouette. In the room's waning light her body glowed, and the only break from neck to waist in the ivory symphony were the dark-nippled, firmly jutting breasts.

She re-hooked the bra, face averted, picked up her dress and reversed it from its inside-out condition. She sounded a little breathless as she slipped it back over her head. "Satisfied?"

"Almost. I want to look at your scalp."

"Then come and look at it," she said wearily and sat down. In ninety seconds he had satisfied himself that there were no more scratches or abrasions hidden beneath her hair than there had been beneath her clothing.

He returned to his chair, and his voice was abrupt. "I don't know why you want me on your side. I don't know what you've got in mind, but let me tell you something I've got in mind. I wouldn't want to find out later that you had a partner and that he had the scratches."

She sounded honestly curious. "And if you did find it out?"

"We wouldn't need any police." The sound of his voice hung in the room, flat and deadly. "I'd break your back. His, too."

"I wish I knew you better, Johnny. Anyone who can make a statement like that, which should sound merely theatrical, and make it so impressively lethal—"

He refused to be distracted. "Who killed Sanders, Lorraine?"

The face she turned to him was perfectly guileless. "I don't know. I didn't see him killed. I'm not sure I know anyone with a good motive for killing him."

"Why were you over there near his place?"

He could see her jawline ridge itself prominently. "That's my business."

"You said a minute ago you needed me," he suggested softly. "I don't move very fast up a one-way street. I want

60

to know what you know. Now, not when it's too late. Let's hear something."

"You've heard all you're going to hear from me," she replied positively.

He did not want an open rupture—yet. He went off at a tangent. "You know a guy named Ed Russo?"

"Russo? I don't believe so. Why?"

"He has an office over at the hotel. He's a slim, dark, slick-looking job, thin face, good clothes, quick way of moving. Was Ellen carrying a white kitten when you saw her last night?"

"Why, yes, she was. I remember it on her arm—"

Johnny nodded. "She had it at the hotel, too. This morning I overheard this Russo asking if a kitten had been delivered for him. I got curious and went upstairs and poured a little kerosene on him. He exploded all right, but not in a way that meant anything to me. Then in his desk I found a newspaper folded back to the Robert Sanders headline."

Lorraine Barnes frowned. "Your general description . . . Does he wear a ruby ring?"

"Never noticed."

"The rest of it sounds like a man named Winslow I see in and out of Mrs. Sanders' office all the time. Hair plastered down—"

"Tight," Johnny agreed. "You know his first name?"

"I think it's Edward, though that doesn't sound—" She looked up at the ceiling. "Edmund. That's it. Edmund Winslow."

"At my place he's Edmund Russo. He worked for Mrs. Sanders? Or was there something personal between them?"

"Something personal? I wouldn't think so." Lorraine Barnes said it slowly; obviously the possibility had not occurred to her before. "And he did run around a bit with a girl in the office. Roberta Perry; everyone calls her Bobby. I know they've dated."

"You got an address for this Perry girl?"

"It's in my address book. I'll get it for you before you go."

"What about her? How would you size her up?"

"Well, a little on the shrewd side, I'd say. Attractive. Calculating is the word I want, I guess. I wouldn't think vicious."

"She'd better be shrewd if she's taking on Russo."

"You don't like him?"

"We've agreed to disagree."

61

Her smile was surprising, the first real smile he had seen on the usually guarded face. "You said he exploded? I don't see any marks on you."

"I must outweigh him seventy pounds."

The smile still lingered. "Years ago I found the application of strength and leverage a fascinating subject. You'd never think it to look at me, but I'm a phys-ed grad." She looked at him steadily. "If we can't be partners, Johnny, how about an armed truce?"

"Why can't we be partners? Because I want to know too much? I want to find this guy."

"I'm afraid you'll have to forgive me if I don't want you finding him at the expense of shattering the foundations of my life."

"Look, Lorraine. I don't give a damn about your private life. I want to know what you know that'll help me get closer to this guy. I don't see why you're afraid—"

"I'll tell you why I'm afraid," she interrupted firmly. "In the important area of the police I'm not yet involved in this thing. If I should tell you my suspicions, and you acted upon them without proof, we would both be involved with the police, and my entire purpose would be defeated. That's why I'm afraid."

He stood up and turned to the door. "Good night, Lorraine."

"Good night, Johnny. I'm sorry."

On the stairs he paused; one of the reasons you'd just about scratched this woman from the derby, Killain, was because you thought she couldn't have the strength to kill Ellen. Now she's a phys-ed grad.

So where are the marks?

He shrugged and ran lightly down the stairs to the street.

CHAPTER 7

JOHNNY SAT SLUMPED in the deeply cushioned armchair in his room and frowned down at his shoes propped up on a hassock. His shift had just gone off and it was time for bed, but an underlying restlessness clawed at his nerves. His physical batteries felt overcharged.

He removed his feet from the hassock, kicking it to one side, and bent down and untied his shoelaces. He toed his shoes off, unfastened the two top buttons of the uniform jacket, jerked loose the tie and undid the constricting collar button on the white shirt. He recognized wryly as he did so that the gesture was superficial; the tension was within, not without.

He tried to relax in the depths of the chair, but the muscles in chest and stomach and thighs crawled and jumped in cramped mute protest at the enforced inactivity. With no conscious volition he found himself on his feet, and he impatiently finished unbuttoning the jacket and slid out of it. He stripped off tie, shirt, trousers and underwear, and in his socks padded over to the bed. Ridged muscles leaped in back and shoulders as he leaned forward to turn down the coverlet and top sheet; he stared down at the bed for a moment and then walked to the window. He raised the shade and looked out; in the early morning light the street below was still deep in shadow, but across the way the upper stories of the taller buildings gave off a golden approximation of the sunrise as reflected from hundreds of windows.

Johnny grunted, half aloud. Live in the concrete canyons anywhere below the twenty-fifth floor and get your sunrises secondhand. He turned away from the window. On the other hand, Killain, he reminded himself, in your time you've seen a few sunrises you'd trade even up for the artificial gold-on-glass brilliance across the street. The wheel does come full circle, but high or low on the arc a man gets restless.

He wandered uneasily around the room in a stocking-footed shuffle; in the corner by the bathroom door he looked down at Sassy, curled up in a tight white ball in the sleeping basket he had gotten for her. He broke off his aimless prowling to walk into the bathroom and splash water upon face and upper body; toweled off, he returned to the bed and sat upon its edge. He reached absent-mindedly for a cigarette from the pack on the night table and then decided against it.

And with no absent-mindedness at all he reached for the phone. "Sally? Afraid you might have left already. Come on up."

63

"Mmmmmm? Business meeting?"

He could hear her initial surprise, followed by the impish humor he had come to expect of her. "Yeah."

"Shall I bring my notebook?"

"I don't need to hear the minutes of the last meeting to know where we left off." He could hear the smothered whisper of her laughter in the phone. "Hustle it up."

"Yes, Galahad."

He replaced the phone, lifted his legs and swung around as he stretched out on his back. For a man who lived by life's tactile sensations there weren't many superior to the feel of clean linen on flesh. He closed his eyes.

When he heard her footsteps in the corridor outside he slid from the bed and had the door open with himself behind it almost before the faint sound of her knock had died away. Sally slipped quietly inside, and he closed the door again. "Mornin', Ma."

She turned. "Well!" Her palm cracked smartly on his bare flesh. "Business meeting! Didn't your haberdasher tell you those socks don't match the rest of your outfit?" The big arms encircled her, and she squealed as her breath abruptly departed. She flinched as his lips descended upon an ear lobe, and in his arms he could feel her knees lifting instinctively. "H-hey! That tickles!"

He released her, and she smoothed down the rumpled front of her dress; as always, her clothes looked too large for the doll-like body. She looked at him speculatively. "This means you're not coming by the apartment this afternoon?"

"Few errands to run, Ma." He returned to the bed, and in seconds she slithered in beside him, the boyish slimness cool to his hands. She stretched lazily along his length, and the little hammers started to pound behind his eyes. Over her shoulder he could see the added light in the room as the golden reflection moved farther down the windows across the street.

He counterbalanced Sally's leaning figure with his arm as she stretched for cigarettes and lighter on the night table. She leaned over him as she flipped on the lighter for the cigarette she popped between his lips. "You know, man—"

"Mmmm?" He blew cigarette smoke up at her.

"You're something better than a vacuum." She grinned down at him. "To accentuate the positive, sir, you're adequate." She punched him in the ribs with a sharp-knuckled little fist and slid from the bed before he could grab her. "I've got to make like a lady again and get out of here."

He could hear the rustle of her clothing as she dressed. He ducked as ash from his cigarette dropped on his bare chest; he brushed at it hastily, rolled sideways and stubbed out the butt. On his back again he locked his hands behind his head and stared up at the ceiling. "Sally?"

"Yes?"

"You know the big blonde down on the mezzanine works for Ed Russo?"

She appeared beside the bed to look down at him, her hands busy with the belt of her dress. "Mavis? A bleached iceberg. She's no more a blonde than I am. A hard ticket. A twenty-minute egg." She smiled wryly. "So I'd like to have her figure. All I know about her is that if you follow the panting tongues there's Mavis. What's on your mind, besides lechery?"

"Information."

"I'd guess that if you didn't run out of money too fast you might get a little."

"From the sound, she better not ask you to hold her coat. She footie-footie with anyone around here?"

"I hear Marty Seiden makes a pass every once in a while."

Johnny's head came off the pillow. "Marty? The kid's over-matchin' himself puttin' on the gloves with that trumpet."

Sally laughed. "Is that my cue to ask you how you know? Maybe he's just apprenticing; a boy has to start somewhere, doesn't he? If you're serious about wanting information why don't you talk to Mike Larsen? He knows everyone. Everyone's business, too."

"Mike?" Johnny nodded slowly. "I should have thought of Mike. Score one for your side, Ma; remind me to put you on the pay roll. That might be—" He trailed off, lost in thought.

"Let me get out of here," Sally said firmly. She bent swiftly and brushed his cheek with her lips. "Don't get up. I'll scout the corridor." She blew him a kiss from the door as she closed it softly behind her.

After staring at the closed door a moment Johnny considered the ceiling again. This Russo, now; he was beginning to have a rather strong smell. There were a few things he'd like to know about Russo. Russo had a distinction: he

65

tied in to both Ellen Saxon and Robert Sanders. No one else with his nose above water did. Except Lorraine Barnes, Johnny reminded himself wearily. He wished he could make up his mind about Lorraine Barnes. She certainly had plenty to cover up cross-town if she'd just come off a date with Sanders before he caught the four in the head. And why else would she have been there? Unless to pour a little lead herself? Maybe Sanders had given her the checkered flag, and she wasn't the type to take it without a rebuttal?

He half rolled over to reach for a cigarette. This Lorraine—

He winced as the phone on the table went off practically in his ear. He grabbed at it before it could ring again. "Yeah?"

"This is Sally, Johnny. I'm calling from the booth in the lobby downstairs." He could hear the bubbling excitement in her voice. "I didn't use the elevator coming down just now, of course, and when I crossed the mezzanine I saw Mavis in her office. This early, mind you." She paused dramatically. "This'll kill you; you know who's with her? What's the name of that cute-looking detective who was here the other night? The one that was around with Dameron when we had the trouble before?"

"Rogers?"

"That's the one. I couldn't think of his name. What do you suppose—"

"He still up there?"

"He hasn't come down the stairs. I can't see the elevators."

"Hang up, Ma. I want to talk to him. I'll call you." He broke the connection on his end and jiggled for the operator. "Public stenographer's office," he told her when she came on the line.

"I doubt there's anyone there yet—" He could hear her ringing. About the fourth ring the phone was picked up; the strident female voice sounded annoyed.

"We're not open yet. Who is this?"

Johnny made his voice neutral. "Let me speak to Detective James Rogers."

"You've got the wr—" The line hummed emptily for an instant. "Detective?" It was almost a gasp. The voice was fainter; she must be staring at Rogers over the lowered phone, Johnny thought. "You're a detective? Why, you no-good—"

66

Johnny replaced the phone quietly. He sat and looked down at it, then shook his head and grinned unwillingly. No place to hide on this one. Jimmy Rogers only had to get to the switchboard to find out where the call had originated. And after having a brick like that dropped on him there was a fat chance of his not checking.

Johnny shook with silent laughter; he could picture Rogers in the middle of the stairs, too mad to wait for the elevator. He got up and went to the closet and shrugged into a robe; from the refrigerator he removed a can of orange juice, punched it open and poured two glasses. He carried a glass to the door and listened. It was not a long wait.

When the footsteps he could hear in the corridor halted outside Johnny opened the door left-handed and pushed the glass of orange juice into the hand upraised to knock. The hand closed around it automatically. "Good morning, Jimmy. Join me?"

Detective Rogers snorted. He was hatless, and the sandy hair stood up in spiked tufts; his smattering of freckles was nearly lost in his high color, and his breath came rapidly. He looked down unbelievingly at the glass in his hand; he half raised it as if to throw it, then changed his mind. He pushed inside, and his voice was throaty. "What in the star-spangled damn hell were—"

He foundered on Johnny's upraised palm. "Easy, boy. Easy. Whyn't you let me know you'd come socializin'?"

"Socializing!"

"Why, sure." Johnny looked surprised. "If you weren't there as Detective Rogers? You go for those big blondes? I ought to tell your wife."

"Blondes? Wife?" The sandy-haired man breathed deeply; his voice geared itself up from sputtering inquiry to authoritarian roar. "Now listen, Killain—"

"Okay, okay," Johnny broke in. "I dropped a shoe. Sue me."

And he started to laugh. He stood in the middle of the floor and laughed until he doubled up helplessly; he shook until he hung helplessly over the back of the armchair, holding his sides. He straightened finally, wiping his eyes, ribs hurting. Across the room Jimmy Rogers, though still red in the face, was fighting to prevent the upturn at the corners of his mouth. He gave up finally and let the meager smile crack through; he looked down again at the orange juice in

67

his hand, lifted the glass and drained it. He rubbed his chin unbelievingly. "Boy! Talk about being struck by lightning! That woman knocked my hat off and jumped on it."

Johnny's internal trembles threatened him again. "Cut it out. I'm sore now. What were you doing down there?"

"Never mind that. What made you call?"

"I wanted to talk to you. How was I supposed to know you weren't there officially?"

"How did you know I was there at all?"

"Do I ask you how you know what's going on around the precinct house? This is my territory. I'll give you a tip, though—it's your fatal beauty. You're too good-looking for the detective business. Go out and get your nose broken a few times. Any woman that ever saw you can spot you at five miles on a rainy night." To retain the initiative he continued quickly. "You probably weren't even makin' a dent in that glacier, anyway. You scoutin' Russo?"

The detective looked at him carefully. "Why should I be scouting Russo?"

"Couple of murders. He's at the head of my list."

The slender man shook his head. "He didn't kill Sanders. He's ironclad on that one."

"So how ironclad is ironclad? Who's his alibi?"

"You know better than to ask me that. He satisfied us."

"He may have satisfied you. He hasn't satisfied me. The same guy killed them both." Johnny paused. "Or don't you characters think so?"

"There could be a difference of opinion. Let me ask you this—what's your interest?"

Johnny opened his mouth, closed it and started over again. "An intellectual exercise."

The hazel eyes measured him. "Cuneo turned in a bad report card on you, Johnny. My name's not Cuneo, but I'm warning you—be careful. I mean it. If you get caught in the machinery you're going to be chewed, and Lieutenant Dameron won't lift a finger."

"An' whatever gave you the idea I'd ask Joe Dameron for the right time, even? He's so square you can cut ice with the edges, and I don't mean it as any compliment, either. I told him where to head in twice a month for three and a half years; you don't need to worry about me runnin' to him. I wouldn't give him the satisfaction."

"I'm not worrying about anything, Johnny. I'm telling you

don't get caught in a rowboat with a canoe paddle. I know that you feel personally involved; it makes no difference. I'll charge this one this morning to one of those days, but I don't want to see your tracks anywhere in the neighborhood I happen to be from now on."

"You own the town?" Johnny bristled. "I thought you were a right guy, Jimmy. You're gettin' to sound just like the rest."

"Just so you listen to the sound, Johnny."

Johnny drew in his breath, but his explosive comment was stifled by the ring of his phone. He looked at Detective Rogers and picked it up a little gingerly. "Yeah?"

"This is Lorraine, Johnny. Hope I didn't wake you. I forgot to give you Roberta Perry's address last night."

"Oh. Yeah. Shoot."

"It's 219 Vernon Street. It's—"

"Right. Thanks. I'll be talkin' to you later." He hung up under the bright-eyed inspection of Detective Rogers and shrugged. "Newspaper boy. Wants my version on the double-header."

"I hope you know better than to threaten the police department with the newspapers, Johnny."

"Threaten? You can only threaten someone who's already scared. Isn't that right, Jimmy?"

Tight-lipped, the slender man walked to the door and turned with a hand on the knob. "Remember," he said and departed.

Johnny rinsed out the orange juice glasses and retired thoughtfully to the bed. He had a lot to think about. He thought about Lorraine Barnes, but his mind drifted to Detective Rogers. He smiled; he would have given a hundred dollars to see the look on Jimmy Rogers' face when that platinum blonde took out after him.

The laughter struck at him again, deep inside. It clawed at him internally; he rolled over on his side and stuffed a corner of the sheet in his mouth to control the smothered yips.

Exhausted, he wiped his eyes; he sighed deeply, turned onto his stomach and fell asleep between two ragged breaths.

Johnny stepped out of the cab and looked up at 219 Vernon Street. It was a tenement neighborhood; he absorbed the dreary and depressing sameness as he crossed the sidewalk. A tired hedge bordered the bumpy, flagstoned walkway from the street to the building whose yellow brickwork presented a sooty, brindled décolletage.

He pushed open the street door and bent to look at the mailboxes. He caught the name at once—PERRY, R. 2-B. So there you are, Killain. Find her at home and get her to talk. Nothing to it.

He tried the inner door and found it locked. At least it wasn't the type of place with free wheeling access to anyone. He rang the bell and had to ring it again after an interval before it was answered by a red-faced woman in a baggy apron, with her graying hair caught up in a kerchief. She had a broom in one hand, a degree and a half from the ready, and as she opened the door a cautious six inches Johnny found himself under the careful scrutiny of two washed-out blue eyes. The woman didn't say a word.

"Miss Perry," Johnny said into the little silence. "2-B."

"She expectin' you?"

"Not today, maybe. Insurance man."

The flat blue eyes looked at him. "You're no insurance man." It was an unimpassioned statement of fact.

"Maybe I should have said insurance investigator."

"Maybe you should have." The look enveloped him again. "Investigator, maybe. Salesman, no. With that face, mister, you couldn't sell cut-rate dollar bills." The broom pivoted as she swung toward the stairs he could see behind her. "Bobby!"

He could hear high heels overhead. "Yes, Mrs. Carson?"

"Man here to see you says he's an insurance man."

The voice upstairs was doubtful. "I'm not expecting . . . what's he look like?"

"Face like a broken-down roller coaster," Mrs. Carson replied promptly. She favored Johnny with an unexpectedly amiable, gap-toothed smile. "Looks like he's lost about three more fights than my Charlie."

"Well, send him on up," the voice said. "I'll take a look." The high heels retreated.

"You heard her, bud," Mrs. Carson said briskly. "Second floor on the left at the top." She opened the front door wider and pointed to the stairs with her broom. "She'll let you in."

"You guarantee it?" Johnny asked her as she closed the door and received the wide-spaced smile again.

"Confidentially, she goes for big men."

Johnny climbed the stairs in silence as Mrs. Carson turned away from him to the back of the building. At the top of the stairs he saw at once that it was going to be a very circumspect audition. Roberta Perry was behind the second door on the left, all right, and the door was open on the chain latch a conservative three-quarters of an inch. Through the narrow opening he could get an impression only of dark hair; he noticed that there were two chains on the door—one below the other, one dull and tarnished, one shiny and new. He wondered when Roberta Perry had put on the new chain.

"I don't know you," the voice said positively.

"We can fix that," Johnny suggested. "The password is Ellen."

There was a little silence. "What about Ellen?"

"Listen, Bobby," he said rapidly. "We can't talk like this. Go in and call Lorraine Barnes and tell her a guy named Killain's on your doorstep. Ask her to describe me, and ask her anything else you want. Then let's see if we can't talk."

"I don't have time." Indecision had crept into the voice, though. "I have an appointment. . . . You know Lorraine Barnes?"

"Call her. Then give me five minutes."

"Well—" Curiosity struggled with doubt. "I'll be right back."

He retreated the width of the corridor, where he braced himself with a bent knee and a heel on the wall behind him and lit a cigarette. He savored the smoke and looked appraisingly up and down the dingy hall. He wondered about a girl like Roberta Perry living in a place like this—not that he'd ever seen her, but her job must pay pretty fair money. . . .

She was back at the door. "She doesn't answer. She's not at the office, either; I tried there, too." The doubt had returned to the voice, intensified.

Johnny moved quickly away from the supporting wall. "Look, what do I have to do? This is important. Lorraine's about forty, dark hair going gray, blue-gray eyes, a little heavy in the superstructure, good legs. Her husband Vic's short and stocky, high color, thin hair combed—"

"Come on in." He could hear the chains rattling, and she opened the door. Inside, he nodded at the linked metal.

"How come the armor plate?"

71

"It's that kind of neighborhood, mister." The reply was pert, and so was Bobby Perry, Johnny decided. She was a short girl, tending to plumpness. The features were good, and the coloration, but the small mouth was petulant, and the chin dropped away fast. She wasn't unattractive, though; the dark hair was cut in a short bob that managed to fluff out wildly all around her head. Her movements were quick; she looked like the type of girl the boys would flock around at a party.

She led the way into her living room, sparsely furnished with mismatched pieces. She turned to wave him to a chair and caught his look. "Sit down. Don't let the props depress you. I have other uses for my money."

"Like clothes?" he suggested, eying her. Her dress was not off a rack, and it did something for her. With her soft-bodied fullness of figure she needed something done for her.

"If that's a compliment I accept it." She smiled as she looked him up and down. "No shortage of material when they had you on the ways, huh?" The smile died, and she looked at the watch on her wrist. "So what's important? You've got to make this quick. I left the office to keep this appointment. You can sit right over there, Mr.—"

"Killain," he supplied again. He walked to the indicated chair, a huge, high-backed, overstuffed relic of an earlier day. It was placed with its back to the large window through which the sun slanted obliquely, and in the instant before he seated himself Johnny had a quick impression of surrounding tenements, flapping clotheslines and rusting fire escapes. He settled back in the sunken depths of the old chair and decided that Roberta Perry had legs a notch or two above the utilitarian class. "I used to be married to Ellen Saxon, Bobby."

It surprised her. She stared at him, adjusting her ideas of him. He could see that she was not sure she approved of the situation. "How long ago?"

"Five, six years."

"Oh. Well?"

"You worked with her. Anyone on her back?"

He could see her relax. "I'm a mercenary soul, Mr. Killain. What's in it for me? And now that I think of it, what's in it for you? Better give me the big picture."

"I'll give it to you quick. I want to find him."

72

"You're the neanderthalic type? It's uneconomic." She bit her lip thoughtfully. "Can I offer you a beer?"

He was surprised. "Sure—"

She was looking at her watch again. "One quick one." She rose from her chair and half turned to the glassed-in china closet behind her, then turned back to him. The plump features were serious. "This noncommercial kick you're on—it's permanent?"

He studied her. "You got something to sell?"

"I didn't say that." She opened the door of the china closet and removed a thick-glassed stein. She pointed it at him. "But if I did have, do—" Her voice trailed off in a ragged gasp, and then she screamed piercingly. She drew back her arm as if to throw the glass, and he ducked instinctively since she was looking right at him. Then the world blew up behind him.

Sharp, repeated sound filled his ears, and the glass doors of the china closet dissolved shatteringly behind Roberta Perry. Her scream flatted out gratingly as she was smashed back into the debris, where she was pinned helplessly an instant before she slid slack-kneed to the floor in another welter of crashing crystalware.

On hands and knees Johnny reached her side, but the first look was enough—the recently admired dress was now torn, stained, and ugly.

In a scrambling, crablike scuttle he got back to the window behind his chair. The large lower pane was completely gone, blown into the room by the bullets fired from the fire escape beyond. He looked out and down cautiously and saw the final hinged portion of the rusted metal which hung suspended ten feet above the alley bed below swinging lightly to and fro from the released weight of the departed caller.

He came back into the room, looked down once more at the body of Roberta Perry and picked up the telephone as he heard the first hurrying footsteps out in the hall.

CHAPTER 8

Johnny lay flat on his back on the sofa in Vic's living room, his shoeless feet dangling over the sofa arm at one end and a pillow beneath his head. His brightly flowered sport shirt hung carelessly from the back of a nearby chair, and a bourbon highball rested on his undershirted stomach. In the apartment's sticky heat Lorraine Barnes sat in the armchair opposite him with her bare feet neatly drawn up beneath her. A duplicate highball rested on the table beside her chair, and she listened with head thrown back and eyes closed to the rumble of Johnny's recital.

"—pinwheels went off all over that place when they got there and found me in residence. Cuneo especially was so mad he couldn't make sense; he didn't want to believe my story even when the lab boys supported it by findin' the scuffed-up rust on the fire escape and the ejected shell cases in the alley below. Then it turned out that a couple or three people in the neighborhood had actually seen the guy gettin' down the fire escape. Even had descriptions. 'Course the descriptions don't tally—they never do at a time like that—but the consensus seemed to favor a stocky guy in gray trousers, a cap and a loud checked jacket. The police—"

Lorraine Barnes opened her eyes, which looked darker than normal in the pallor of her face. "A loud checked jacket?" she interrupted. "And a cap? In all this heat? Do you go to commit a murder in an outfit like that?"

"You think he was tryin' to look like someone else?"

"Certainly trying not to look like himself. I wouldn't give that description houseroom." She sighed and passed a hand over her eyes, then twisted in her chair to try for a more comfortable position. "If this heat would only let up I might be able to think." Her voice was husky; she smiled wanly. "I'm beat, I admit it. Right down to my socks, if I were wearing any."

"They gave you a hard time?"

74

"Oh, not by their lights, I suppose. When Rogers got here he had just two questions—had I been here, or where had I been, and did I have any witnesses? When I had no alibi for the time Bobby was killed I received the magic carpet ride downtown. That Rogers is polite enough, but in his own way he's as much of an earache as Cuneo. I don't like them—either of them." Conviction strengthened her tone momentarily and then died out as heat and weariness took over. "I have the most dreadful feeling I'm doing this all wrong, Johnny. The original decision seemed simple enough, but now it's complicated beyond belief. That girl—" Her voice trailed off as she sat huddled in the chair.

"Whyn't you talk a little bit about what happened over at Sanders' place that night, Lorraine? Might take a little pressure off you, if nothin' else."

Her lips firmed stubbornly. "I know nothing that would help you."

Ice cubes tinkled in his drink as he leaned up on an elbow. "How do you know, for God's sake? More important, how do I know? This is personal with me, Lorraine. I'll find out anyway, but you could save me leg work. An' time."

For an instant he thought his savage probing had made an impression, but then she shook her head. "I can't trust your reaction."

"What do you care about my reaction?" he began quickly, then paused. It was the wrong thing to have said. Obviously she did care, or she would not be balancing on a high wire with the police. He groped for a saving phrase, but she spoke before he could get himself back on the rails.

"Why do you think Bobby Perry was killed, Johnny?" Her voice was subdued.

He sank back on the sofa. For a moment he had been close to something, but the moment had passed. "That kid had hot little hands for money. She was workin' up to something with me. She could have been tryin' to peddle something to a guy allergic to buying. Or she could have been someone's alibi for Sanders, and the someone fixed it for good that she wouldn't change her mind. I kind of like that one."

He lifted his head again to finish off his drink, set the glass down on the floor and swung his feet around from the sofa arm and into his shoes. He stood up and picked up his shirt from the back of the chair; he looked down at the

75

drawn-faced woman. "One thing you can bet me—she knew who it was. She'd left work to keep an appointment. The guy set her up like a clay pigeon, climbed the fire escape from the alley, didn't see me in my high-backed chair and closed the books on her proposition."

"You think it's Russo, or Winslow, or whatever his name is, don't you?" she asked, watching him closely.

He shrugged. "I'd like to find out Roberta Perry was his alibi for Sanders. For sure that'd put him on my hit parade."

"I can't see him as a murderer," she said slowly. "From the little I've seen of him, that is. Although do you ever really know? This man didn't start out to commit three murders. One thing just led to another." She paused as she thought of something else. "Are the papers going to know you were in that room when Bobby was killed?"

"The police don't want it given out, but the landlady at least knew it. They muzzled her, or they think they did." He tried to make his voice light. "How about it, Lorraine? Just the answers to a coupla questions?"

"I'm sorry, Johnny."

Despite himself his voice thickened and his hands hooked into claws. "Lorraine—"

"Stop it." Her voice had gone cold as ice. "I know you'd like to muscle it out of me, but I wouldn't recommend it."

He could feel the heat in his face; not trusting his voice he turned and walked from the apartment, only with an effort preventing himself from slamming the door. He stormed down the single flight of steps and out onto the walk. Damn all stubborn women . . . how was he going to get it out of her, anyway? He jerked open the iron gate and clanged it shut behind him as he turned right to walk back to the hotel. He almost bumped into a figure that detached itself from the fence. "Got a light, bud?"

Impatiently he reached for the lighter in his shirt pocket. He looked at the lean, dark face in the lighter's glow, a dark suit, complete with jacket, even in this heat. And then the dark man's right hand flashed up and caught Johnny solidly under the left ear and rocked him sideways into the iron fence. He bounced off into a left to the body that was partially minimized by his nearness as his lighter clattered to the sidewalk, and the dark man spoke raspingly. "Maybe you'll mind your own business after this, bud."

76

The dark man launched another right hand, but Johnny partially blocked it, caught the hand and dragged the body behind it in close. He hurt his own right hand on the belt buckle of the dark suit, and the man sagged, gasping. Johnny picked him up bodily by the shoulders, carried him over to the fence, and hung him by his coat collar from a blunt iron pike.

"Now, punk," he growled throatily. "Who sent you? Start talkin' and save yourself a little wear-and-tear." He slapped the dark face hard, left, right, left, right. The suspended man's toes scrabbled on the sidewalk as he tried in vain to get leverage. Dimly Johnny heard a car door slam and the sound of running feet; he turned to confront the two shirt-sleeved men coming at him shoulder to shoulder.

"Get him!" the nearer man grated, and a bludgeoning arm and the weight of the blocky body thrust Johnny backward. Instinctively he clamped the thrashing figure in his arms, and as he drew on arm and back muscles for the constriction he half turned to look for the third man. Metal glinted to Johnny's right as the man in his arms bleated hoarsely, screamed and went limp; he shifted position, but not in time. A starburst exploded above his right eye; he felt something rip, and a curtain of blood washed over the eye. He threw the crumpled body in his arms to the sidewalk, where it rolled off into the gutter, and turned to the man with the brass knuckles.

He absorbed a body punch as he cocked his head awkwardly because of the blindness in his eye; he moved in closer and landed a glancing left of his own. As the man backed up a step Johnny charged him; the shirt-sleeved arm swung hurriedly and missed, and Johnny dumped him to the sidewalk with a blasting right that missed the chin and landed on the throat. With bitter anger a brassy taste in his throat he stooped and picked up the crawling figure waist-high and slammed it into the street.

"All right, Johnny. That's enough." Johnny whirled at the voice behind him, half crouched, arms outstretched, and the speaker backed hastily away. "Easy. This is Rogers." Johnny focused with difficulty on the sandy-haired detective and then looked beyond him to the man still suspended from the fence.

"Outta the way." His voice was a croak. "I want that one."

"Stop it!" Detective Rogers grunted as Johnny shouldered

through him on his way to the fence. He reached quickly for his shoulder holster as Johnny grabbed the belt of the dark man on the fence, and yanked. The man came off the fence wearing just the sleeves of his suit jacket, and his face was a dirty gray.

"Let's hear it while you can talk," Johnny snarled down into the face, and his shoulders swelled as his arms bunched. "Who sent you?"

Detective Rogers pushed in between them; his face was shiny. "Drop him, Johnny. I'll handle this."

"Aghhhh—" The sound was prolonged, breathy, and disgusted. "Take a walk around the block, Jimmy. Then you can have him."

"I said drop him." Firmness had returned to the detective's tone; he placed a hand on the dark man's arm. Johnny snorted angrily but turned loose his belt hold, and the dark man's dead weight nearly carried Jimmy Rogers to the sidewalk with him.

Johnny stepped back and sleeved the obscured eye, but it filled right up again, and he reached for the spare handkerchief in his hip pocket.

"Johnny!" Lorraine Barnes ran toward him awkwardly; in her dash to the street she had lost a shoe. Her breath came rough and hard as she turned indignantly to Detective Rogers. "I saw it all from—upstairs. They were waiting, one at the—gate, two in the car. They rushed—"

"I saw it, too," the detective cut in. He looked down at the man at his feet. "I couldn't've been more than sixty yards down the street, but by the time I put in the squeal from my car and got over here Johnny had rearranged the landscape." He looked down at the revolver still in his hand as though wondering how it had come there; he re-holstered it hurriedly. He took three steps to the curb and inspected Brass Knuckles, who was struggling to his knees. The detective pushed him to a sitting position, took one look at the still figure in the gutter—the man who had been in Johnny's arms—and turned away.

"Your eye—" Lorraine Barnes said to Johnny.

"I'll run him over to the hospital soon's the boys get here," Detective Rogers said quickly.

"No hospital," Johnny said flatly. He turned to Lorraine. "You don't mind my drippin' a little I'll go upstairs and clean up."

"You're going to need stitches in that eye cut," Jimmy Rogers said positively. He stepped out into the street with his arms over his head as he pushed his way through the gathering crowd and signaled to the muted siren and flashing red light which had turned into the end of the block.

"Come on." Johnny took Lorraine's arm and walked her back through the gate. She hobbled along beside him in a one-shoe-on-and-one-shoe-off gait until she retrieved the lost pump at the upper end of the walk. She pulled back to look at Johnny doubtfully as she slipped it back on her foot.

"He said you needed stitches, Johnny—"

"He been right about anything yet? Let's get upstairs."

Upstairs, she took charge briskly. "Lie down on the sofa," she told him as she picked up the phone in the hall. "I'll be right in with towels."

He pulled off the shredded, blood-streaked shirt and stretched out carefully. His ribs were throbbing. There was a gaping rent in the thigh of his slacks; he probed at it, but the damage seemed to be external. He tried to regulate his breathing to minimize rib pressure and listened to the cool voice on the telephone.

"—rush, Terry. I want the strongest non-prescription external coagulant that you have, material enough for a couple of cold compresses, a little extra gauze and some thin tape. You'll hurry it, please? Thank you."

She came in almost at once from the bathroom with a wet and a dry towel. "Now let's have a look." She swabbed delicately at the right side of his face, cleansing the cut area, and leaned down to examine it critically. "Just above the brow. More of a deep bruise than a cut, although it is split. It undoubtedly should have a stitch or two. It could scar without it."

"It could scar with it, too." He looked up at her curiously. "You a nurse?"

"I was." She turned his head to one side. "You're bleeding under the other ear, and there's a lump."

"That's from my friend on the fence." He straightened his head to look up at her again. "Forget the stitches. Slap a little tape on it."

She looked doubtful. "If I can stop the bleeding. The boy should be here any second now; the drug store's just up at the corner." She rose at a knock on the door. "There he is."

It was Detective Rogers who walked into the room when

79

she opened the door, but the delivery boy was right on his heels. The sandy-haired man stood silently as Lorraine Barnes opened the package, made one quick trip for an antiseptic and cuticle scissors and deftly worked the coagulant into the split brow. She tidied up the bruised edges of flesh, cut thin strips of gauze for a pad, and overlaid it with a professional-looking application of tape. She stood up and brushed off her skirt. "I'll make a compress for that lump under your ear."

She went back into the bathroom, and Jimmy Rogers stared after her an instant before he looked down at Johnny. "Acts like she knows what she's doing. Put a knife in your teeth now and you'd be ready for the photographer." His voice turned official. "What started this fracas?"

"You said you saw it."

"I know what started it downstairs. How about before that?"

Johnny's voice was unpleasant. "If you hadn't stuck your beak in so damn quick I'd have found out."

"They'll talk," the detective said, but there was no conviction in his tone.

"They'd have talked to me. Another forty-five seconds and I'd've had his life history."

"Another forty-five seconds and I'd have been taking you in for manslaughter," Jimmy Rogers said sharply. "People become deceased when you bust them all up." He stared moodily downward from his height. "I begin to see what the lieutenant's been talking about all these years. What makes you tick? By God, I thought I'd seen a few tidal waves—"

He broke off as Lorraine Barnes returned with the compress and adjusted it along the jawline and under the ear. Johnny grinned up at her as she straightened and wiped her hands on a piece of gauze. "Call Gus at the hotel for me, huh? Tell him to run up to my room and get me a change of clothes from the skin out and shoot it over here in a cab."

She nodded, and went back out to the phone. When she re-entered the room her lips were curved upward in a smile. "He wanted to know how badly you were hurt this time."

"Sounds as if he knows Johnny," Detective Rogers said dryly. He adjusted the set of his shoulder holster inside his jacket and looked down at Johnny on the sofa. "I'll be running along. Be a little careful where you get your exercise."

"What did he mean by that?" Lorraine asked curiously when the door had closed behind the slender man.

Johnny stretched carefully. "That's just his way of tellin' me not to go lookin' for the guy that sent the muscle. He's warning me not to let him catch me jumpin' on someone's foot." He fingered the lump under his ear. "He thinks I need to look."

"And you don't?"

"You're damned right I don't. I racked this boy Russo up the other day, so here he is, in spades. This time I'll braid his tail for real, only it's got to be a little private, with Jimmy watching from the sidelines." He looked at her appraisingly. "You happen to wonder how come he was outside where he had a ringside seat for the corrida?"

"Why, no—" Her eyes narrowed. "He was watching me?"

"Or me. Could've followed me over here. Maybe it's seeing us together gives him an itch. Jimmy's a good boy. Don't underestimate him." He made his voice casual. "Which brings us back to why it'd be a good idea for you to un-button a little about what happened the night—"

"That's enough, Johnny." She cut him off. "We've been all through that before, and the answer is no."

"I could get tired of workin' a one-way street," he told her softly. "I've told you things you'd have had trouble findin' out. I'm closer to things than you're likely to be. You're Vic's wife; I'd like to steer you right on this—"

He stopped when he saw her expression; he knew that he had said the wrong thing again. "You're not here because I'm Vic's wife," she said flatly. "You're here because you think I have information that you want. Whether I do or not is problematical, but I've told you before and I'll tell you now for the final time. I'm not about to let you pull the house down around my ears because of your own personal involvement!"

The heat in her tone fanned his own fire; for an instant he balanced on the razor edge of forcing the issue to a showdown, before belated common sense came to the fore. *She knows, Killain, and you don't. She may not know the murderer, but she knows more than you do. You cut yourself off from the possibility of learning what she knows, and you've bitten off your nose to spite your face. This is a strong-willed, determined woman.* He spoke abruptly. "How about me takin' a shower?"

"If you keep your head dry. I'll get you towels."

Under the steaming hot water he soaked the mounting ache in his bones, and in the mirror he inspected the brass-knuckle-raised purple welts under his ribs. He dried himself carefully.

Lorraine tapped on the bathroom door. "The cab driver brought your clothes," she called. "I put them in the bedroom."

He felt better after the shower. In the bedroom he dressed hurriedly; he wanted to get back to the hotel. He transferred money, keys and wallet to the fresh slacks and made a little bundle of the fragments he had removed in the bathroom.

"New man," he announced upon re-entering the living room.

Her eyes were speculative. "From personal observation I don't believe there was very much the matter with the old one." She continued before he could take advantage of the opening. "You know you're going to have a head like a gourd in the morning?"

"Maybe I should take a little something to justify it?"

"I wouldn't recommend it." Her inspection of him was deliberate. "If you're mad I hope you don't stay mad. I do need your access to information."

"Well then, why—"

"Because the situation almost certainly calls for halfway measures, and you don't know how to use them. As you just proved out on the street."

Johnny boiled out the door without even saying good-by; he simmered down a little during the cab ride back to the hotel, but he was still under a driving head of steam when he entered the lobby and approached the bell captain's desk.

"Thanks, Gus." He raised his eyes aloft. "Russo around?"

Gus crooked a finger across the lobby. "In the bar." The dark-eyed glance lingered on the patch over Johnny's eye. "You and Russo?"

"Not yet." Johnny crossed the lobby rapidly and felt a sense of release at the sight of Ed Russo in the third booth from the door, sitting across from a big man in a light-colored, wide-brimmed panama. He walked down to the booth; anticipation was so strong he could taste it. The semi-public nature of the scene concerned him not at all; here was the man. He placed both hands on the table edge, leaned forward slightly, and waited.

Ed Russo looked up carelessly from his lowvoiced conversation; the thin mouth tightened, but he did not break off until it became apparent to him that Johnny had no intention of moving on. "What the hell, Killain?" he demanded forcefully. "This is a private conversation."

Johnny considered the dapper man; it was not the reaction he had expected.

Russo was addressing his companion. "This is the guy I was telling you about that tanked me, Tim." He turned back to Johnny, eyes on the brow patch. "For you, I hope it's nothing trivial, mister. All your troubles should be major." His voice sharpened as the bitterness showed through. "I got fifty bucks right here says you can't take me again, wise guy."

Johnny blinked. He sends three goons to entertain you, and now he wants to bet you fifty he can do it himself? Whoa, Killain. Wrong script. Back up and get a fresh start.

Russo was getting impatient; the lean, arrogant features were poised upward. "Well, sonny boy? I'll take you for fun, money or marbles."

"You couldn't take one side of me," Johnny growled, but the riposte was mechanical. To himself he was forced to admit that Ed Russo's response seemed genuine.

The dapper man flushed darkly; he started to rise. "Right now I'll show you, hot shot. Out in the alley."

The big man across the table from him put a hand on Russo's arm; he spoke for the first time. "Business before pleasure, Ed." He sounded quite jovial; Johnny looked at the expensive dark brown gabardine slacks and the cream-colored sport coat; the man had a round moon face and a livid scar that pulled down a corner of the heavy mouth.

"You're right," Russo was saying in evident disappointment. He sat down again slowly. "Not tonight." He looked up at Johnny. "But any time after tonight. Any time at all. Right, Tim?"

Tim looked at Johnny; he removed a fat cigar from his breast pocket and rolled it lightly between his palms. "He looks healthy to me, Ed. What makes you think you can take him?"

"You think I can't?" Russo was angry again. "I'll bet you fifty, too. I never saw a bull like that I couldn't take!"

"You know I ride with you, Ed." The big man said it soothingly; Johnny thought that he had never heard a deeper

83

voice than the big man's heavy resonance. "Does it hurt to mention the guy must weigh as much as I do?"

"I don't care what he weighs. I won't be half splashed the next time he takes his sucker shot." He rapped impatiently on the table with the bottom of his shot glass and looked around for the waiter. "Come on. Let's have one more drink and get moving."

He had so obviously dismissed the interruption from his mind that Johnny straightened a little self-consciously; as he backed away uncertainly, until he stood with his back to the bar, Russo and the big man were again engrossed in earnest conversation.

Johnny tried to make up his mind—was Russo conning him? Somehow he didn't think so. Yet if Russo hadn't sent the goon squad, who had? Johnny shook his head, which ached. Maybe a drink would help his muddied thought processes; he left the bar to go upstairs, conscious of a massive letdown sensation.

In his room he already had a drink poured before it occurred to him he hadn't seen Sassy. She couldn't hear him come in, but the vibration of the floor under his feet always brought her trotting. He made a quick circuit of the room and the bathroom without finding her. Had she gotten out somehow? He dropped to his knees and grunted with relief when he saw the fluffy mound under the bed. "Come on out here, you," he ordered her. "Where's that welcome I always get?"

She stared out at him, and, vaguely uneasy, he reached in for her. She didn't want to come; she hooked her claws into the rug in protest, but there was no real fight in her. He lifted her out and looked in alarm at the dull eyes and the drooping whiskers; he placed his palm lightly on the small pink nose. It was dry and hot, and even the usually lively tail hung limply.

Johnny made a hurried round trip to the refrigerator and tried to tempt the kitten with a sliver of shrimp. Yesterday she would have taken shrimp and a finger to the first joint; now she lay motionless after one apathetic sniff. He sat back on his heels and looked down at her with concern. "What the hell, baby doll—you're sick."

She tried to crawl back under the bed, and that decided him. In the yellow pages of the phone directory he ran down the list of names, looking for the one he wanted. Kendrick

84

. . . Lacy . . . Landry. Landry. Jeff Landry. He reached for the phone on the night table.

"Landry Cat and Dog Hospital—sorry, we're closed," a woman's voice announced in a parroted gabble.

"Let me talk to Jeff Landry."

"I'm afraid he's too busy to come to the phone right now—"

"Tell him it's Johnny Killain."

The line hummed, and he waited impatiently. "Johnny? Is it really you?"

"Yeah, Jeff. Fine friend I am, only callin' you when I need a favor. I know it's after hours for you, but I got a sick kitten here. Be a good guy an' let me bring her over?"

"Johnny Killain with a sick kitten? It beggars the imagination. Come to the back door."

"I'm halfway there. Put some beer on the ice."

In the closet he found an empty shoe box which seemed large enough. He punched several pencil holes in each end, put Sassy into it and put on the cover. The kitten made little effort to fight off even this indignity, and Johnny left the room hurriedly.

In the lobby he ran into Mike Larsen. "Buy you a drink, Johnny?" Mike looked at the tape decorating Johnny's forehead. "What happened to you?"

"Tripped on the top step. Listen, Mike. Ed Russo's in the bar, third booth from the door. Take a look at the guy with him and see if you know him. I'll be back in an hour, and you can buy me that drink."

Going through the foyer doors he was whistling for a cab.

CHAPTER 9

THE REAR OF THE LONG, low building on the side street was dark, but Johnny's knock was answered almost immediately as Jeff Landry opened the door himself, hand outstretched. He practically dragged Johnny over the threshold with the vigor of a grip surprising in a man of medium size.

"Johnny, you bandit! Wonderful to see you again." Jeff Landry was a slender man casually dressed in khakis and tennis shoes. His hair was ash-blond and close-cropped, and horn-rimmed glasses tended to minimize but not wholly conceal the impact of a face of quiet strength. The mouth and chin were firm to the point of being stubborn.

"I'm not much of a neighbor for a guy who lives just cross-town, Jeff. In the cab I was thinking how the neighborhood here had changed since I'd seen it."

"More than you think." Jeff Landry tapped the box under Johnny's arm. "Let's have a look at the patient. We can talk later."

Johnny followed the veterinarian through a semi-dark maze of tiered wire cages and runways; an occasional yelp or bark disturbed the quiet, and Johnny could feel a slight scrambling in the box under his arm as the variegated smells filtered through to the kitten. There was a musty, animal odor in the air, overladen with a piny tang, and an antiseptic pungency which increased in strength as they moved to the front of the building.

He blinked at the dazzling fluorescent light which flooded the white formica-topped tables and the chromiumed instruments in glassed-in cabinets ranged around the walls of the examination room into which Jeff led him. An assortment of odd-looking machines with dangling electric cords took up most of the working space on the metal coverlet that hinged down over the double sink with its gleaming faucets and rubber hoses trailing down to the tiled floor.

Johnny looked around him and whistled softly. "You sure have improved things, Jeff." He tapped the examination table lightly as he placed the shoe box upon it. "Looks like you could take care of me on this thing."

"Too good for you." Jeff Landry's voice was matter-of-fact.

Johnny laughed. "I know you better than to think you're kiddin', too." A dozen years ago in northern Italy he had seen Jeff Landry charge a squad of soldiers abusing a mongrel dog. Jeff had needed help, but not a great deal; the white heat of his anger had dissolved the would-be sadists like melted butter.

He watched as Jeff drew on a pair of forearm-length gloves; the vet removed the cover of the shoe box, and Sassy stared up at him apprehensively. "A Persian, Johnny? You're traveling in class."

"She adopted me. She's deaf as a mackerel, Jeff."

The blond man lifted Sassy from her box; the kitten made no struggle, although the small ears were flattened to her skull. "It's not unusual; about sixty per cent of the purebreds are deaf. It's a mutation attributable to the inbreeding which produces the coat and eye coloration." His eyes never left Sassy as she crouched flat on the formica surface of the table and hissed halfheartedly at the gloved hand exploration.

"You mean if she didn't have the blue eyes she wouldn't be deaf?"

Jeff Landry removed the glove from his right hand and dexterously pried open the kitten's mouth; her back arched as she started to resist, but he had accomplished his purpose and released her before she could successfully mount her opposition. "I didn't say that." He turned to remove a small thermometer from a graduated rack. "Her eyes could be bronze and she could still be deaf. It's how the lightning strikes. What do you feed her?"

"Oh, shrimp and liver and milk, mostly. Little chopped beef once in a while."

"How much do you feed her?"

"I usually just cover the bottom of a saucer."

The veterinarian shook his head. "How often?"

"Pretty often, I guess," Johnny admitted. "She seems to be hungry all the time. Until today. What's the matter, Jeff?"

Jeff Landry's voice was patient. "The matter is that I strongly suspect that all that ails our patient is a muddle-headed case of overfeeding. Reason is not given to these little articulated minuscules, Johnny. Just because you feed her today, she can't be expected to remember that you'll do so tomorrow. She'll eat herself bowlegged every chance you give her. I'm sure that you've been forcing as much on her in twelve hours as she needs in seventy-two, and a great deal of it too rich. I'll keep her overnight and make out a diet for her. She may not be as happy at mealtime, but she'll be healthier."

He picked the kitten up with the re-gloved hand, and Johnny followed him out of the examination room's glare to the gloom of the cage walkways. He watched Jeff open the door on the top left of a tier of small cages and put Sassy inside.

"She'll be fine here tonight," Jeff said. He moved on toward the back. "Come on. I've got a little refrigerator out here I keep drugs in. And beer."

He kicked a kitchen chair in Johnny's direction in the small room that housed the refrigerator and a battered desk. He uncapped two bottles of beer, and Johnny dipped his head hastily to sip off the overflowing collar from the bottle pushed across to him. Jeff picked up his own bottle and swallowed twice; he lowered the beer and looked over at Johnny as he perched himself on the edge of the desk. "I'll probably have a new address the next time you come calling."

"You're moving? How come? You sunk a lot of money in the place. I thought you were satisfied."

"I am satisfied." The blond man stared at his beer. "I'm getting squeezed. You remarked yourself how much the neighborhood had changed. My little place is practically lost in all the new buildings that have gone up around here. I'm in the seventh year of a ten-year lease, but my landlord has been pushing me for a year to take a settlement on the lease and move to another address. I kept telling him that due to zoning restrictions I'd have to move so far my business couldn't reasonably be expected to follow me. I kept telling him, but he kept pushing me."

"So you got the lease. Let him push."

Jeff took another swallow of beer. "I wonder. Lately it's been second-hand, and a little ugly. About six weeks ago a lawyer came to see me. Really a type. Said he represented an outfit who had made a deal to finance a new building for the landlord, and I was the only thing holding up the deal. He asked me to set a figure on a lease settlement, and I did, finally. You can't fight city hall forever. I might have had a little balloon in the figure I gave him, but not too much, so when this character offered me half and told me to take it or leave it I got a little sore. I threw him out. He made a few noises on the way to the effect that I'd be glad to settle for less than that before they'd finished with me."

"So they started to muscle you around?"

Jeff hesitated. "Not in the way you would think. I believe they're behind what's been going on, but it's been so devilishly clever—" His voice trailed off. He jumped up from the desk and began to pace the room's narrow confines. "I'm sure, Johnny, and yet I'm not sure." He gestured impatiently. "Three weeks ago a woman brought in a thoroughbred Scottie for a bath and a clip. Twelve hours after she left it here the dog died. Of poison."

Johnny sucked in his breath. "A slow pill."

"I have to think so. The dog didn't get it here. The woman raised particular hell—charged negligence, malfeasance and all the rest of it. I carry liability insurance, naturally, and the company paid off. Last week it happened again. A terrier, this time. And a stinking shouting match with the customer out in the waiting room heard by fifteen people. The insurance company paid off again and canceled the policy. The next one's on me."

"Let's go talk to that lawyer, Jeff."

Jeff's smile was rueful. "You wouldn't think I could be stupid enough to talk to him without getting his name, would you? Well, I did. I realize now he deliberately didn't tell me."

"Then let's go see your landlord."

"I've already done that. He denies any knowledge of what's going on, and I get the oddest feeling that he's afraid himself. I told him point-blank I didn't give a damn whether he was responsible or not; I was holding him responsible. I told him that with the next animal that died around here in similar circumstances it was going to be me and him all over the sidewalk. He believed me. He followed me for half a block, bleating that he didn't know anything about it and that he couldn't do anything about it."

Johnny turned it over in his mind. "Rough. It leaves you sitting and waiting for the cloudburst. I don't see what you can do."

"I can close up. And go looking for that lawyer."

"The idea appeals to me," Johnny admitted. He drained off the last of the beer, wiped his lips with the back of his hand and scowled at the empty bottle. "If I was a member of the posse. There's got to be another answer, though, Jeff."

The vet's smile was tight. "You think so? I've had three weeks to come up with one, and I'm not even close. Well, forget it. It's my problem. Another beer?"

"No, thanks. Listen, Jeff. You'll think of somethin'. An' if you think of anything I can do—"

"I wish I could think of something I can do." Jeff picked up the empty beer bottles from the desk and returned them to the case on the floor, his mind obviously not on what his hands were doing. "If I don't call you, Johnny, you can pick up the kitten tomorrow."

89

"Oh. Yeah. Listenin' to you I nearly forgot why I was here."

Jeff's smile was less forced. "Come to the office any time after six; that's pickup time. I'll have the diet list ready, too. I'll be busy with incoming animals, so we probably won't get a chance to talk. Take care, boy. *Vaya con Dios.*"

They gripped hands, hard, and Johnny departed by the back door. On the way back cross-town in the cab he went over it again in his mind. What kind of people deliberately poisoned animals to force a man to break his lease? It had to be deliberate. Yeah, but what could you do?

The first person he saw in the lobby was Mike Larsen, and Mike was on his feet before the glass doors stopped swinging. He waved a slip of paper at Johnny. "Been watching for you."

Johnny turned the telephone message over; the time stamp on the back said 9:35 P.M. The message was brief. "Call Dameron."

He looked at his watch. 10:12. "Any ideas, Mike?"

"Not a one. Unless there's a story goes with that patch on your eye?"

"Not for Joe. Jimmy Rogers was right there. Well—"

"Here." Mike handed him a dime. Johnny walked to the pay-phone booths in the corner of the lobby and stared musingly at the scribbled phone numbers on the booth wall after dialing. What—

"—precinct, Donovan."

"Lieutenant Dameron."

A wait. "Lieutenant Dameron's office—Rogers."

Johnny cleared his throat and pitched his voice up. "This is Mavis, Jimmy."

The pause was fractional. "Get on over here, Johnny."

His eyes narrowed. "Are you askin' me or tellin' me?"

"Why, we're asking, you delicate flower." Detective Rogers' tone was syrupy.

"What's it about?"

"There's an easy way to find out."

The connection was gone. Johnny opened the booth door thoughtfully and shrugged at Mike outside. "They want me over there."

"They say why?"

"Big mystery."

"I'll drive you over. If you're going. My car's outside."

Johnny hesitated. "You goin' that way anyway?" He had

90

ridden with Mike before; Mike Larsen drove a car like the devil was at his throatlatch. "Well, okay." He debated a moment. "You think I should call Lorraine first?"

"Lorraine?" There was no mistaking Mike's curiosity.

"No real reason," Johnny said a little vaguely. "She and I've been tradin' light jabs with the big gloves. I can't get her to level with me. Still, if she knows somethin' I can get her to tell me I'd just as soon not walk in on Joe Dameron stone cold. I think I'll call her." He fished a dime out of the change in his pocket and returned to the booth; Mike lounged in the open door. The phone rang and rang, and Johnny hung up finally. "Nobody home."

"Maybe she went out to a movie to cool off," Mike suggested. "That apartment gets like an oven sometimes."

"Yeah," Johnny agreed absently. The unanswered phone reminded him of another caller who had been unable to reach Lorraine—Roberta Perry. Lorraine hadn't been back to the office since the murders, still you couldn't catch her at home. So where was she spending her time?

He followed Mike out through the foyer. The sporty little MG was on the restricted side of the street; Mike fished a press card out from under the lowered visor as he got under the wheel. "That's for the cruisers," he told Johnny. "The beat man knows the car."

"Must be nice to be a big shot." Mike Larsen laughed as he started the motor; Johnny listened to the rough roar of the engine and raised his voice to make himself heard as their quick start snapped his neck. "Take it easy in this spittoon, now; I could shot-put this thing across the street."

Mike stopped for the Seventh Avenue light and turned to look at him. "I took a look at Russo's client in the bar. Knew him the minute I saw him. Name's Connor, with an *o*, not an *e*. Tim Connor."

Johnny nodded. "Russo called him Tim. What's his action?"

Mike gunned away from the light, beating a cab to the one-lane-wide passageway between the parked cars beyond Broadway. "His action is a little complicated. When I began to think about it Connor and Russo made an interesting combination. I've always wondered how Russo took the kind of living off that balcony that kept him in two-hundred-dollar suits. Maybe I know now."

"Nothing legal, I hope?"

Mike caught the light at Eighth Avenue and thundered into a sweeping right-hand turn; the little car sounded like an engine-testing block as they set sail up the left-hand side of the one-way street. "You could get a debate on that. This Connor is tough, but he's slick, too. It's a combination you don't get too often. He's made it pay off." He settled back in the bucket seat, and the MG skimmed north. "You know this town, Johnny; if you spread a little money around, public relationswise there's nothing you can't do. Connor came up with a refinement."

Mike Larsen took his eyes from the street ahead long enough for a quick side glance at Johnny. "His particular variation on the theme was simple. Instead of building the client up you tear the competition down. The way Connor worked it out it was bad news for the competition."

He slowed in mid-block to catch the change from red to green at Fifty-fourth, accelerated and made a left turn on a wheel and a half as he darted between the curbed cars. Johnny unclenched his hands with difficulty; this Mike really *used* a car.

The MG flew west; Mike had to raise his voice above the muffled roar of the motor. "Like this, Johnny. You and I each own a restaurant, on opposite corners of the street. You're a smart operator, and I'm a shmo. You hire my best waiter away from me, and my hostess, and my chef. All of a sudden you've got the customers and I've got the ulcers. I'm a shmo, see, but now I'm mad."

He swung the little car into the curb, and Johnny looked up at the familiar weather-stained brick building. Mike sat with his hands loosely on the wheel as he continued. "I'm mad, so I make a couple of phone calls. Someone puts me in touch with Connor, and I tell him the story. He says, okay, Pop, how mad are you? How much do you want to spend? I say the hell with the money—let's see a little blood. So in a couple of days a well-dressed couple come into your place at the height of the dinner hour, and during the meal the woman suddenly becomes embarrassingly, deathly ill, without ever getting away from the table. In a roomful of people her escort accuses you of serving tainted food. And three nights later it happens again."

Mike's fingers drummed hollowly on the steering wheel. "And that's only the beginning. You've been doing the right and usual thing by all the visiting fire department boys and health inspectors, but all of a sudden now you pick up two kitchen violations from the health department. Runs to a little money to get the citations lifted. Then a piece of brass walks in from the fire department with a little bad news. Seems as though the guy you bought the place from put in that partition over there without an alteration permit. It's a fire hazard—got to come out, pronto. So it ruins the looks of your whole place? Things are tough all over. Who pays for it? You do."

He lifted his hands from the wheel as he looked over at Johnny. "Connor doesn't appear personally too often. He holds himself out for the big ones, the boffolas, or the ones that take a little finesse. He's got a stable of half the unemployed actors and actresses in town. He has a stiff payroll, but he makes a nice living."

"Seems to me the trick would be to stay alive to enjoy it."

Mike shrugged. "How do you prove that kind of stuff? Regardless of what you suspect? You can't prove a thing."

A little tickle stirred faintly in the recesses of Johnny's mind. Who— He reached for the door handle. "I've got to get inside, Mike." He said it slowly; his mind was still on Mike's parable. Who had said— The tickle died; he had lost the thread. He swung open the door and lifted himself up on the sidewalk.

"You doing anything in the morning?" Mike asked abruptly. "Let's get out on the Sound for a couple of hours."

"In the morning?" Johnny echoed doubtfully.

"Blow the stink of the town off ourselves," Mike urged him. He grinned a little self-consciously. "I'll give you another inducement. I've been trying to make up my mind to talk to you about something. Maybe out on the boat I'll be able to forget I'll be betraying a confidence."

Johnny nodded. "Seven-thirty?"

"Good. I'll pick you up." Mike waved and roared away, and after staring after him for a moment Johnny ran lightly up the worn white stone steps. He nodded to the uniformed man at the information desk just inside the door and turned left and strode briskly along the oil-darkened wooden floors of the station house. At the old fashioned head-high desk he looked up at the uniformed sergeant.

"Killain to see Lt. Dameron."

The sergeant nodded and picked up the phone. He replaced it with the two syllables of Johnny's name still hanging in the air. "Second door on the left."

Detective Rogers was at the opened door; he stood aside to let Johnny enter and closed the door behind him. The cramped, dark room seemed crowded with chairs and with men; the air was stale and blue with cigarette smoke. Johnny ran his eyes quickly around the seated semicircle—a grinning Cuneo, a fat detective with round eyes whom Johnny knew only as Owly, a man he didn't know at all, Jimmy Rogers standing behind him and Lieutenant Dameron behind his littered desk.

Johnny looked carefully at the big, apple-cheeked man with the cropped iron-gray hair and the hard gray eyes who sat plunged into the depths of his swivel chair. The entire room was illuminated by a single gooseneck lamp on the desk. "Kindergarten class, Joe?"

The big man's lips moved; it could have been a smile. "You might call it that. I guess you know everyone here except Ray Hawkins."

Johnny inclined his head in the direction of the cadaverous, rumpled man on the outer wing of the seated men and received fifty per cent acknowledgment. Ray Hawkins had baggy, dark brown pouches under his eyes, and directly above them the eyes themselves looked like two hard-boiled eggs.

"Ray works out of here, too," the lieutenant said. "He and Owly caught the squeal on Sanders, which makes 'em high men on this totem pole." He squashed out a cigarette in his ash tray and removed a fresh one from the pack in his shirt pocket. He leaned back in his chair when he had it lit, the solid-looking face expressionless. "Show him what we have for him, Jimmy."

From behind him Detective Rogers pushed into Johnny's hand three or four double-spaced typewritten sheets, stapled together; the red-line-left-margined legal-sized crisp stationery was doubled back to a prominent signature on the right-hand side of the upmost sheet, trailed on the lower left by additional signatures.

Johnny looked at the prominently isolated signature, and a cold little wind blew down his back. *Victor Barnes.* His voice was harsh. "What's this thing supposed to be?"

"Forgot you couldn't read." Johnny's eyes swiveled; Ted Cuneo was smiling at him. Unpleasantly. The lean detective was obviously delighted to explain. "It's a confession, Killain. Signed. And witnessed."

A pulse hammered in Johnny's temple. "Confession to what, you damn hyena?"

The smile disappeared; Cuneo stood up. "You know what. To the murder of Ellen Saxon. I had a talk with your boy."

Johnny's eyes flicked back to the papers in his hand. The signature of the first witness was Theodore Cuneo. The confession fluttered floorward as Johnny's hands balled; his chin came down on his chest, and his weight advanced to the frontal arches. His voice sounded as though it originated outside the room. "You dirty little wart, Cuneo!"

"Head him off, Jimmy!" Lieutenant Dameron rapped out the order, and Jimmy Rogers dropped both hands down on Johnny's rigid right arm.

"Stop it, Johnny!" Detective Rogers' tone was sharp as his feet left the floor; something in the urgency of the sandy-haired man's voice penetrated Johnny's red haze and halted the independent action of the right arm upon which the detective's weight rested. Jimmy Rogers was looking at Ted Cuneo, and his voice was curt. "I could let him go, Ted."

"So let him go." Detective Cuneo's tone was bitter, and his features were brick red. "A real wise guy. Let him go." He darted a sullen glance at the silent lieutenant. "Christ! How does a burn-up like him live so long?"

Detective Rogers snorted. "If you'd been with me a little bit earlier tonight you'd have a better idea."

Ted Cuneo scowled, hesitated and finally sat down again. Jimmy Rogers released his hold on Johnny's arm and stepped back. Johnny looked around again at the varying expressions in the semicircle, and finally he nodded. "Okay, boys. I read you now. Too many blips on the radar for a minute. You don't think it's legitimate, either. I'd never have gotten within a thousand yards of a confession like this if you thought it was worth a quarter." He took a deep breath, and his eyes came back to Cuneo. "Vic Barnes is my friend. I'd just like to find out you went in there and roughed him up, you needlin' little moron—"

Ted Cuneo soared up out of his chair and landed crouched forward, feet apart. His face was scarlet. "Just let me catch you spitting on the sidewalk, even, Killain!"

Johnny cut across the shrill vehemence. "Don't try it alone, man. Not ever."

Lieutenant Dameron's big hand crashed down on his desk as papers flew. "That's enough of that! You're no privileged character, Johnny. Keep a civil tongue in your head."

Johnny shifted from his eye-to-eye exchange with Cuneo and stared at the apple-cheeked man behind the desk. "So how come he confessed to something he didn't do, Joe?"

The lieutenant's voice was patient. "He called out to the turnkey and asked for a stenographer, said he wanted to dictate a statement. We sent one in, and he did. You saw it."

"With no pressure at all? Did he have any visitors?"

"No visitors. And no pressure, despite our comedian here." Cuneo flushed a dull bronze. "Entirely voluntary."

"Voluntary, hell! If he didn't have visitors, he was reached some other way. A message, a note, maybe. It could still be in there with him. Why don't you guys get off your butts and shake down—" The cumulative dead-pan stare from around the group finally penetrated his intensity. "All right," he said shortly. "You already did it. So what'd you find?"

Lieutenant Dameron lifted a small green blotter from his desk; beneath it was a crumpled, torn-off corner of brown wrapping paper. "Don't touch it, Johnny."

Johnny walked around the desk and looked down at the crudely lettered penciled message: YOUR WIFE IS NEXT, BARNES.

"Came in on his supper tray, he says." It was Detective Rogers' voice; Johnny was still staring down at the note. "Folded into his napkin. I talked to Finnegan, in the cell block. Barnes has been having his meals sent in. I've already been across the street." He shrugged elaborately. "Nothing."

"Of course you realize you could be telling him something he already knows, Jimmy," Ted Cuneo said morosely.

Johnny ignored him. "Vic thought Lorraine would be safer if he confessed. Which is what whoever sent the note wanted him to think."

"This Lorraine." Lieutenant Dameron's hard gray eyes bored up into Johnny. "I know she hasn't told us all she knows yet. I don't think you have, either." Johnny was silent, and added color crowded up into the red face measuring him. The big man bit his words off between tightly compressed lips. "Has Lorraine Barnes told you anything she hasn't told us?"

"How should I know what she told you? Do I get to read

96

the transcript? You got to come crying to me because you can't run your business?"

The hands on the desk top knuckled slowly. "Three people have died. The interrelationships are complicated; the lives of more might be threatened, yet to satisfy a whim of your own you're prepared to sabotage justice. If I ever find out that you withheld information—"

Johnny's neck swelled in its suddenly too-tight collar. The desk creaked as his weight crowded it. "Ahhhh, bag it, Joe! Sabotage justice! If I had one-tenth the information you do-nothings had I'd be so close to that rotten weasel you could smell him sweatin' from here. And when I found him—" His clenched fist smashed down on the desk; a stapler jumped up in the air, tottered on the desk's edge and fell to the floor. The room was very quiet.

Lieutenant Dameron stood up behind his desk. His voice was level, positive. "Your attitude proves my point for me. I thought I'd give you one more chance; you've had it. I'll put what I've got to say now in the form of an order." He leaned forward as he emphasized each word. "You stay away from everyone connected with this case in any way, shape or form. If I find you've contacted anyone like you did the Perry girl I'll get you off the street if I have to get a law passed."

Johnny felt the hot blood in his face; his arms flexed involuntarily. "You think you're God Almighty, Joe? Go play with your wooden soldiers. Why should I listen to you?"

"Because I say so!" It was nearly a shout; the bull neck was thrust forward.

Johnny looked at him. He turned his head and looked at the smirking Cuneo, at the round-eyed Owly, at the grinning Hawkins and lastly at the expressionless Rogers. He turned silently and walked to the door; it shivered on its hinges from the smash with which he slammed it shut behind him.

CHAPTER 10

Johnny dropped the empty buckets at the foot of the standpipe at the shore end of the elongated pier and fumbled in his hip pocket for his wrench. He glanced out over the Sound's blue-green chop, already turned brassy in the early morning sunlight, and knelt on the scarred, splintered planking, warm to the touch, as he opened the cut-off valve at the base of the pipe.

As he filled the buckets he could see Mike in the cockpit of the thirty-foot cruiser dancing heavily at the end of her lines a hundred feet out on the pier. Amidst the small forest of stubby masts and tired rigging in the dingy hulls around it Johnny could make out the semicircled brass lettering on the bobbing stern: *Ye Olde Beaste, NYC, NY*. Mike had the cowling off the brutish-looking engine and was probing its interior with a long-necked oilcan.

Ye Olde Beaste was a marine monstrosity. Its beam was out of all proportion to its water line, so that even in a flat calm it floundered like a dish in a bathtub. It made a good fishing platform, but there its virtues ceased. In addition to its disproportionate beam-to-water line difficulties, *Ye Olde Beaste's* seagoing life was further complicated by its engine. The perverted sense of humor of a former owner blessed with more money than brains had caused him to install in the boat's plumply pedestrian interior a power plant barely short of Gold Cup standards. Its weight guaranteed a stern-heavy sag and a steady shipment of spray aft. The engine was Mike's pride and joy, despite the fact that it was a tricky assignment to keep the monster throttled back to the point necessary to prevent hull and engine from going their separate ways.

"Catch, Mike." Mike straightened from his loving inspection of the engine; he accepted the filled buckets as Johnny backed down the top rungs of the wooden ladder spiked to the pier piling and swung them off the planking over his

98

head. Mike passed up two empties and sleeved his brow with the forearm of his gray sweat shirt.

"It's a hot one, boy."

"Gonna be," Johnny agreed. "We'll catch exercise today, period. This sun's gonna drive 'em too deep for our surface stuff."

"Ahh, it's a change from the asphalt, anyway. You ready?"

"Soon's I fill these and get the ice out of the car." Johnny climbed back up on the pier, returned to the standpipe, filled his buckets and re-closed the cut-off valve. He left the buckets and walked off the shore end of the pier to the MG parked in the weeds at the end of the graveled road. He could feel the heat of the planking through the crepe soles of his sneakers, even this early in the morning; at the car he removed from the floor a fifty-pound piece of ice wrapped in a sodden newspaper and swung it up to his left shoulder. He could feel the wet trickle of the melting ice run down his back as he retrieved the buckets, passing one up to the extended left hand which balanced the ice.

At the boat he set down his liquid burden and passed the ice down to Mike; he heard it thump down into the box as he reached back up over his head and handed down the water pails. He dropped down to the deck himself from the ladder after casting off the lines and fended off from the pilings with the boat hook as Mike started the engine with a deep-throated roar that sent the nearby gulls zooming aloft.

They crept away from the dock and out into the deserted Sound, and Mike nodded at a sleekly expensive cabin cruiser which contrasted sharply with their own weather-beaten down-at-heels appearance. "I'll own one like that in a year, Johnny."

Johnny looked at the cruiser and back at Mike. "You plannin' on hitting the sweeps? Besides, you couldn't desert the old lady."

Mike smiled. "I'll retire the old lady and keep her for a pet."

Johnny crouched before a compartment door in the cockpit and removed a tangle of gear. Swiftly he assembled two spinning rods and sorted out a double handful of mismatched reels, swivels, lures, leader wire, a battered knife and a rusty hatchet. Beyond the point the breeze freshened; *Ye Olde Beaste* lumbered through lengthening swells, and the air had a crisper tang. Johnny removed half a dozen bottles of beer from the case in the bottom of the boat and put them in the box with the ice.

"Any place in particular you want to try?" Mike asked from the wheel.

"Anywhere—I don't care. When you get tired of burnin' gas, throw over the float." He bent double to peel his T-shirt off over his head, and Mike grimaced at the Indian-bronzed torso.

"Wish I tanned like that. Last time we came out here I nearly burned right up; some deficiency in the skin pigmentation, Doc Phillips says. On the water I've got to keep covered up. How about breaking out a sandwich? I could eat a rubber boot."

"A beer, too?"

"Later, maybe."

They gnawed on thick slabs of ham and cheese inartistically thrust between jagged slices of rye bread. Mike tossed his torn-off crusts to the trailing cloud of gulls, stood up and brushed off his hands, and reached down to cut off the engine. In the sudden silence they began to lose headway, and he catwalked up to the bow and tossed over the float anchor which would keep them headed steadily into the wind.

Johnny drew a deep, satisfied breath. The sun was hot on his back and chest, but the breeze was cool. He handed Mike a rod as he returned from the bow, and they settled down in silence on opposite edges of the cockpit rim. The loudest sound in the boat was the slap of the choppy little waves under the bow. With the teamwork born of long practice they alternately cast and reeled, cast and reeled, and for forty-five minutes an occasional grunt and the low whine of the gear was the only medium of exchange.

Mike stacked his rod finally, butt down in a homemade holder, and reached for his cigarettes. "Not a minnow in the North Atlantic." It was an uncomplaining statement of fact; he shielded his lighter against the breeze, puffed on his cigarette, pulled his cap farther down over his eyes and propped his back against a stanchion. Johnny tried one more cast, reeled in and stacked his rod beside Mike's. He stepped over to the icebox and removed and uncapped two bottles of beer.

"Sure wish old Vic was out here with us," Mike said as he accepted a chilled bottle.

"Yeah," Johnny agreed. "Mike?" Mike widened half-closed eyes. "This Tim Connor—"

100

"Yes?"

"How come he can keep on cuttin' the mustard on a spread like you were tellin' about last night?"

"I'd say it was a combination of things. Some people never even wise up they're being targeted. The ones that do can't prove anything. And even if you got him or some of his people dead to rights on a job, it would probably still be borderline if it was criminal. Tim keeps a couple of two-bit ward heelers on his pay roll, and they help to tone down the occasional beef."

Mike stared out over the blue-green-gold Sound, his shoulders swaying slightly with the movement of the boat. "I first ran across Connor three years ago. Friend of mine asked me if I could get Connor off his back. My friend was an insurance man, and a couple of years before that he'd been from hunger. Then it was laid in his lap that for a price he could get a listing each month of all the claims paid by one of the largest health and accident insurance companies headquartered in New York."

Johnny frowned. "Claims? What good—"

"I guess you never had a health and accident policy." Mike grinned. "Or never had to collect on one, if you did. It's a little tricky; you never get what you think you have coming. No outright misrepresentation: it's just that the fine print really pares away what the blurbs advertise. So if you're up for a settlement and you find that such-and-such is disallowed in Clause thirty-two, and that so-and-so is unfortunately excluded in Clause forty-four, why you're a little unhappy about it. Usually it would end right there, but now here comes a subscriber to the Connor service ready, willing and able to sell you *his* policy. With the head start he has on knowing your settlement, after listening to your squawk very sympathetically, how much trouble do you think he has getting you to cancel the policy that let you down and take out a new one with him?"

"A little sharp." Johnny's tone was thoughtful. "It doesn't sound illegal, though. Why'd your friend want out?"

"Because as far as Connor was concerned what he was doing wasn't illegal, but the same couldn't be said for my friend. The insurance companies have a word for that little bit of business. They call it 'twisting,' and if you're reported, and it's proven, you blow your ticket. You're not allowed to approach a potential customer and suggest or recommend

101

that he cancel an outstanding policy and rewrite the same thing with you. If the customer told his own agent you'd wind up in the commissioner's office."

"So you tell the customer to keep it under his hat."

"Sure you do, and when you're hungry enough you'll gamble that he will. You'll risk it. But then the day comes when you're not hungry any more, or not that hungry. Do you always know to whom you're talking? You've got something to lose now, and finally you say to yourself the hell with this noise. I can use a little sleep nights. And the next time the man comes around you say, thank you very, very much, sir; it's been a real pleasure knowing you. And that's the day you make a painful discovery."

"You can't turn loose of the wildcat?"

"Exactly. The man carefully points out to you that while his service might be viewed as a bit unethical, the hook is set a little deeper in your mouth. You have a license to lose, and a backlog of people on your books any of whose reminiscences in the wrong place could have you up before the mast."

"What happened to your friend that wanted out?"

"He's still taking the service. I went around to see Connor, and he read me a nice little lecture on minding my own business. My friend bought another Cadillac the other day. I figure he's earned it. He's my age, but I flatter myself he looks ten years older."

Johnny rubbed his chin. "So now we have Ed Russo tied in somehow to a character like this Connor. Did you know Russo was dating this Perry girl who was killed?"

"He was? You mean Ed ties into that public relations office, too?"

"Spent a fair amount of time over there, according to Lorraine. Not under the name of Russo, either. The point is this, though. This Perry kid would have blackmailed the Pope if she had a thirty-seventy chance. I figure whoever killed her did it to keep her mouth shut because of something she knew. The day I was there she said—"

"There?" Mike interrupted. "Where?"

"I was with her in her place when she was killed."

"You were what?" Mike's inflection was strangled. "The papers didn't—"

"That's right. Dameron must've muzzled 'em. The girl's landlady knew I was there; Joe must've put her on ice. The killer shot from the fire escape over a high-backed chair with its back to him. I was in the chair. 'Course I never got a look at him because by the time I got to the girl on the floor and back to the window and the fire escape he was gone."

"Bro-ther!" Awe reverberated in Mike's reverent tone. "What did Dameron have to say to that?"

"I was still gettin' the echoes last night. I fouled off a couple of Joe's questions, and he got up on his hind legs and told me one more move from me like that one and he'd personally have me starched an' ironed."

"You'd better watch your step, then. Lieutenant Dameron draws a little water in his section of town. Let me catch up with this. Is Russo your candidate for the Perry girl?"

"Russo's my candidate, period, except that Jimmy Rogers told me he's ironclad on Sanders, and everything stems from Sanders. I'm hoping that Roberta Perry was Russo's alibi for the time Sanders was killed. I'd like to find out. If she was, and the alibi was a phony, he'd have to knock her over to make sure no talkee, or no blackmail."

"Boy!" Mike wagged his head from side to side. "Quiet now while I go back and unscramble this omelet you just dropped on my chin. There's a couple—"

His voice died away meditatively, and Johnny stood up and stepped up from the cockpit and walked up to the bow. He knelt, removed sneakers and socks and rose again to slip out of slacks and shorts. He went over the side in a long, shallow dive and thrashed a headlong hundred yards in a clumsily effective six-beat racing crawl, then rolled over on his back and floated effortlessly, eyes half closed against the sun.

He floated high in the water; an oddity in his chemical metabolism and the concentration of weight in his upper body gave him an unusual natural bouyancy. He could, and often did, swim for hours, and while his inelegantly powerful crawl stroke developed no real speed, he could maintain it almost indefinitely.

He rolled over again and swam back to the boat, shoulders surging up out of the boiling water. Alongside, he surface-dived and swam down under the keel, his eyes open in the cool green underwater shadows. That far down there was a definite chill in depths unwarmed by surface sun. He could see the trailing kelp and the greener marine growth barnacling the squat underside of *Ye Olde Beaste,* and he kicked

103

strongly and surfaced on the far side, blowing a fine spray. He looked up at Mike carrying pails and towels from the cockpit to the bow. "Her whiskers are trippin' her, Mike. The old lady needs a shave."

Mike nodded. "She hasn't been out of the water in eighteen months. I ought to have it done."

Johnny swam lazily along the water line, and Mike tossed him the bow painter. Johnny went up it hand over hand until he reached the brass guardrail; his hands gripping it until they whitened, he doubled up his body and muscled himself aloft in a handstand upon its polished surface. Upside-down-erect, in sheer exuberance he raised and lowered himself three times in elbow bends, corded muscle standing out in forearms and shoulders.

"Monkey boy," Mike's voice drifted out to him. "Too bad I haven't any peanuts."

Johnny hand-walked the rail further in from the bow, and lowered himself to the deck. He sluiced the salt from his body with two upturned buckets of fresh water and dried himself off roughly. He slid into shorts and slacks, spread the towel on the deck, and lay down on his back.

Mike's head poked up out of the cockpit. "You want to try it someplace else?"

"What time is it?"

"Few minutes to ten."

"Maybe we better get back."

He lay and soaked up the sun and considered his present inability to savor this carefree life. Ellen was dead; he had promised himself he would find her murderer, and his lack of progress gnawed at his nerves. He had accomplished little or nothing, and now there was Joe Dameron to contend with also—

Beneath him the deck planking sprang into an independent vibrating life of its own as Mike started up the engine. He throttled it back to a rumbling mutter and stepped up and over Johnny, straddling him as he pulled in the float. Johnny braced his elbows as *Ye Olde Beaste* swung broadside to the swell and began to roll. He opened his eyes at the abrupt sound of Mike's voice. "I want to talk to you."

Johnny scrambled to hands and knees and followed Mike down into the cockpit. Mike advanced the throttle arm slightly, and the motor's mutter changed to a muted thunder; *Ye Olde Beaste* circled clumsily and started on her return

104

trip. Mike's face wore a scowl; his tone was flat and heavy as he raised it above the sound of the engine. "I don't like the sound of what I'm going to say, but I'm going to say it anyway. After what you told me a few minutes ago I think you need this for your frame of reference. Lorraine Barnes —" He hesitated, and Johnny waited. Mike's voice pitched higher. "Did you know Lorraine killed her first husband? Shot him?"

Johnny stared. "The hell she did!"

"She did, all right. Fifteen, sixteen years ago. It was a tight fit for her; she bought the gun she used, and the smell of premeditation was all over it. There must have been extenuating circumstances, because it wound up as manslaughter, and she got seven years. Did about four and a half. Moved away; remarried after a couple of years. Divorced. Moved again, to New York. Married Vic." Mike's eyes swept the Sound as if he were searching for something. "I doubt the police know it; all those years, and a couple of name changes. And she wouldn't tell them."

"But she told you?"

"Me?" Mike looked embarrassed. "No. Vic told me. I guess he had to tell someone to convince himself it wasn't her fault."

"You'd have to say he's convinced, the way he's goin' down the line for her." He blew out his breath; if the police ever took Lorraine's prints—

It wasn't likely that they would, though; she wasn't charged with anything. No wonder Vic had clammed up completely; one or two wrong words from him and the whole apple cart would have been upside down. He probably hadn't trusted himself to cope with police questioning.

The conversation died. *Ye Olde Beaste* plowed steadily shoreward, throbbing in every pore. After a time Johnny stirred himself; he disjointed the rods, rinsed the salt water off them and the rest of the gear and stowed it away. At the dock he helped Mike slide the metal cowling over the engine, and they lashed the canvas cover down over the cockpit. They washed up at the standpipe and walked through the weeds to the car.

It was a quiet ride back to town. Mike dropped Johnny off at the hotel entrance and went on to garage the car. On his way through the foyer Johnny decided on impulse to go up against Russo again. Russo was in some manner tied in to this whole mess. If he could just get Russo mad enough to spill something—

He nodded to Gus behind the bell captain's desk as he crossed the lobby, then ran up the marbled steps to the mezzanine. He opened the door to the public stenographer's office, and Mavis Delaroche lifted her blonde head from the magazine she was reading. Upon recognizing her caller she closed the magazine with a snap and stood up at her desk.

"Well!" she said icily. "Look whom we have with us, unfortunately. Outside, muscles."

"I like you, too, kid," Johnny told her, closing the door behind himself. He looked at her. There was a lot of Mavis to look at; in her high heels she very nearly matched Johnny's six feet, and she was not undernourished. She was tastefully attired in a clinging little number which depreciated her considerable assets not at all. Her skin and eye coloration were those of a brunette, which her platinum crown gave the lie to, but not unattractively. The face was well if largely boned; only the mouth spoiled the larger-than-life cameo. The mouth was tiny and pouted.

"Didn't you hear me?" she demanded. "You're not wanted around here, mister."

"You're breakin' my heart, kid. The weasel around?"

The brightly lipsticked mouth tightened. "I wish he were. He'd fix your wagon for you. You used up all your luck the other day."

"That what he told you? Guess maybe he can sleep better nights if he's convinced himself that's the way it was. You his manager? Do him a favor, kid. Retire him. In that league he's a raggedy canoe in white water."

The red lips curled derisively. "I just hope I'm there to see him take you."

"Yeah? You like a little blood? You musta been in the front row when they were throwin' the Christians to the lions."

"Beat it," she said tersely. "You're excused. You can see Ed's not here."

"Who needs Ed?" he asked her. If he could stall a few minutes Russo might be back. This Mavis was in too much of a hurry to get rid of him. "You're the stenographer around here, aren't you? Or are your duties more highly specialized these days?"

The brunette eyes glittered. "I ought to belt you one myself."

Johnny sighed with exaggerated patience. "Loosen up the spring on that hair trigger, kid. I walk in here like a citizen to dictate a letter, and all I get is a lot of abuse. You're the stenographer?"

"Certainly I'm the stenographer!"

"So take a letter."

She looked at him, hands on hips. "This ought to be good for a laugh, anyway," She sat down and uncovered her machine. "From a speedball like you I'll take it right in the typewriter. Go ahead. Shoot your head off, and I do mean off." She paused and looked up at him suspiciously. "Unless this is a gag?"

"No gag, big stuff. Very serious business. Crank it up." He watched her slip a battered carbon between a sheet of bond and onionskin and wind it into the machine. She looked up at him impatiently.

"Well? Who's it to?"

"To? Oh. Yeah." He looked up at the ceiling for inspiration. "Ready? Today's date, no address, to the New York City Police Department, 240 Centre Street, New York, New York. Gentlemen: I am making this confession voluntarily—"

"Wait," the blonde girl interrupted, whipping the paper out of the machine. "You didn't say how many copies."

"Copies? Two's enough."

She paused in her task of aligning fresh carbon and onionskin, her tone patient, as to a backward child, as she discarded the worn carbon in the wastebasket beside her and brushed off her fingertips lightly. "An original and one copy? Or an original and two copies?"

"I can see this is a complicated business, requirin' steel nerves and lightning-like decisions. One copy."

She discarded a carbon and an onionskin from the sheaf in her hand, reinserted the balance in the machine, typed in the date and salutation and looked up at him. "Go on."

"Gentlemen—" Johnny ran a hand thoughtfully over his chin stubble. "I am making this confession voluntarily and of my own free will."

Mavis half turned to look at him, then ducked her head down and clack-clacked away at the keys.

"I am and have been under no coercion whatsoever to—"

Mavis backed her chair away, her hands in her lap. "What

is this? You going to sign it yourself? And where did a mug like you learn to dictate a letter?"

"We don't all have visible talents, kid. Like you." Johnny leered at her companionably. "And don't worry about the signer. I got him on ice. Let's see . . . under no coercion whatsoever to make this statement. I killed Robert Sanders, Ellen Saxon, and Roberta—"

"You're crazy!" Mavis burst out as her chair again rolled away from the typewriter. "Will you—"

"Will you stop bothering the motorman?" Johnny cut across her eruption. "—and Roberta Perry. I recognize my legal responsibility in the dictation and signature of this confession. Space for a signature; space for two witnesses' signatures. Got it?"

The typewriter tac-tac-tac'd and came to a stop. Mavis reeled the letter out of the machine, removed the carbon and handed Johnny the letter and copy. She tossed the carbon into a folder on her desk and weighted the folder with a fifteen-inch ruler. She picked up a business envelope and typed the address on it; her voice was disdainful as she gave it to him. "You're out of your mind if you think you're going to get anyone to sign that thing."

Johnny looked at her; he felt that somehow she sounded very well pleased with herself. The corners of the small mouth turned downward as though she had difficulty in repressing a smile. She turned her face sharply away when she noticed Johnny's inspection of her; the smugness on her features as she toed her wastebasket under the desk puzzled him. And then suddenly he had a feeling. All his life he had acted on impulse; he reached for the folder beside the typewriter, and sensing his movement Mavis grabbed for his arm.

"Here! What do you think—"

He was too quick for her; her voice was still echoing angrily as the ruler slid into her lap and he picked the folder up and opened it.

"You give me that!" The blonde girl snatched the heavy ruler from her lap, rose with a jerk and pointed it at Johnny. He stared down at the top carbon in the stack in the folder whose glossy, hard-backed surface retained a perfect copy of his dictated letter.

"I can see a man lacks a little something in privacy around here, Mavis. This your own idea?" He began to flip through the carbons in the folder, each a one-time-used perfect impression of a typed letter.

"You get your big nose out of there!" Mavis dropped the ruler on the desk as she came around it on the run. She came like a man, hands doubled into fists, swinging for the body. Johnny caught a flailing arm and spun her in against himself, pinioning her as she struggled within the circle of his arm.

"A nice racket," he said in her ear. "An out-of-town businessman drops in and dictates his bid on a contract, and with a fresh carbon you've got a copy. Whaddya do then? Look up his competition and peddle it to them?"

Her position proved to be a tactical mistake. She lifted a foot and viciously raked the length of his shin with a high heel. She lifted the foot again, but she had his attention now. He dropped the distracting folder and transferred the freed hand to the nape of Mavis' attractive neck. In two long strides he frog-marched her back to her desk, bent her over it, picked up the ruler and solidly swatted the tight skirt's most prominent characteristics. Mavis yelped shrilly and nearly bucked the desk over. Johnny tossed the ruler back on the desk as he let her go, and she straightened up, holding onto herself.

"I hope you weren't wearin' a girdle, kid," Johnny told her. He stooped to retrieve the folder of carbons from the floor. "Shall we call it a draw? I'll show you mine if you'll show me yours." He pulled up the leg of his slacks and looked down at the long scrape on his shin, oozing blood two-thirds of its length. He looked back at Mavis. "Your turn, kid." She stood motionless, hands behind her, two bright, angry tears in the brunette eyes. "Chicken, huh?"

Her voice was hoarse. "You give me back that folder!"

"Later. If Russo gets shook about it, send him around to see me." He looked at her thoughtfully. "Or is this a strictly Mavis Delaroche production?" He smiled at her silence. "I don't know why you rate Ed Russo so high, kid; pound for pound you got better action. Let's see you sit down. You know what the song says—it only hurts for a little while." He turned to the door, then glanced back and waved to the tall girl's still-standing figure. "Think of me when you look in the mirror tonight, kid."

He closed the office door quietly from the outside.

$\mathbf{H}$E WOKE FROM AN UNEASY SLEEP with a long shudder; Ellen had called him. He had heard her so plainly that he half sat up and stared dazedly around the familiar room. He was soaked with perspiration, and his mouth was dry and cottony.

He pushed himself woodenly to the bed's edge, and the hot knife came alive, and bit and twisted. Ellen would never call him again, because he had let her down when she needed him. Ellen, who of all people had deserved a break, and hadn't had one. Her killer was still walking around loose, no doubt planning other murders, and Johnny Killain, who had solemnly promised himself that he would avenge her, was stumbling along in the dark like a blind fool.

He knuckled fiercely at his eyes and stood up. In the shower's hissing water he promised himself all over again. He'd find this killer, wherever he was. And whoever he was. He'd find him, and when he did—

He turned off the water and in the silence stared blindly at the white tiled wall.

Ellen . . .

He leaned against the low counter and watched a dark-haired, white-uniformed girl at the right-hand end of the large desk beyond it. The girl wrote busily, referring occasionally to a little book at her elbow. Johnny glanced behind him; the waiting room of the Landry Cat and Dog Hospital was a beehive of activity. There had been a dozen people waiting in the comfortable chairs when he had arrived, and it seemed to him that two more had since come in for every one who had left.

The desk area beyond the counter was efficiently busy. The girl in front of Johnny was expediting the discharge of the recovered animals; at the other end of the desk a blonde was admitting the newcomers. To the left of the desk was a heavy, paneled door, through which each time it opened came a ringing chorus of barks. With the door closed there was no sound; Johnny realized that Jeff had soundproofed this waiting room, in addition to the money he had spent out in back. No wonder he hated to leave.

A white-jacketed attendant emerged from the back and deposited a black carrying case on the counter in front of Johnny. "That's not—" Johnny began as the attendant turned away, then bent for a closer look. The pink nose and white whiskers crowded up against the neat wire mesh looked familiar; Johnny pushed the tip of a finger through the mesh, and Sassy nipped it enthusiastically.

Johnny laughed. "You've got to be feelin' better if you've got all that ginger, baby doll. Jeff's got you travelin' in style."

"Here's her diet, Mr. Killain." The dark-haired girl handed him a closely written half-sheet. She smiled impersonally and looked for the next name on her list. "Dr. Landry will mail you the bill."

Johnny hesitated, but the girl had already called the next name. He picked up the carrying case, and backed off a few feet. If he knew Jeff Landry there never would be a bill, mailed or otherwise. Should he try around at the back to say thanks? Probably do Jeff no favor, he thought to himself, at the rate people were still coming in. Jeff must be busier—

He heard the voice first; he hadn't seen the big man enter. He must have pushed up to the counter out of turn, because Johnny could see resentment on one or two faces, and there was a hush in the waiting room. Johnny looked at the expensively dressed beefy body, and the light-colored panama with its too-wide brim, at the round moon face and the livid scar drawing down a corner of the heavy mouth. "—tell me why I had to rush over here?" the overpowering bass rumbled through the room.

The dark-haired girl looked doubtful. "You're Mr.—"

"Morton. Charles G. Morton."

Oh, fine, Johnny thought. He set down Sassy's carrying case. Charles G. Morton? The last time Johnny had set eyes on this fine-feathered bird—which had been last night—his name had been Tim Connor.

"Morton?" The dark-haired girl turned over papers on her desk. "Oh, yes." She looked up in sudden uncertainty. "It was Mrs. Morton we called—"

111

"I know, I know," the big man boomed. "Mrs. Morton is a bit indisposed. She called me at the office and asked me to stop by here and see what this mysterious call is all about. Now will you please tell me why I'm here, young lady? I'm a busy man."

There was no mistaking the girl's nervousness. She rose abruptly. "If you will please step inside, Mr. Morton, Dr. Landry will—"

"Young lady!" The girl quailed before the roar. "If Dr. Landry called my wife, will you kindly have him step out here and tell me why? I'm sure the doctor's time is valuable, but so is mine."

The girl was nearly in tears. "He's just inside, sir—"

The big man seemed to swell. "He's as close to here as I am to there. What kind of nonsense is this? You'll have me thinking in a moment he doesn't want to see me."

The girl flew out through the paneled door, and Charles G. Morton leaned back negligently against the counter and half turned to survey the waiting room as if to measure the extent of the audience reaction. His casual glance passed over Johnny, hesitated, swiveled back and focused—hard.

He's coming over here, Johnny thought. Play a hunch. Morton, Schmorton. This water buffalo is up to no good. What have you got to lose? Play the hunch.

Charles G. Morton apparently didn't like loose ends; he moved away from the counter like a man of action. Chest to chest with Johnny, he looked at him scowlingly. "I know you. What—"

He broke off as Johnny shook his head ever so slightly and tapped the carrying case at his feet with his toe. The big man looked down at it puzzledly. "Ed sent me over," Johnny told him, trying to put a sense of urgency into his voice.

The opened mouth snapped shut and reopened. "*Ed* sent you? Ed sent *you?* Am I going crazy?" He tried to muffle the boom of the thunderous voice. "Is this guy off the hook? Has—" He broke off again as the paneled door swung open to admit Jeff Landry.

One look at Jeff's white, strained face was all that Johnny needed to know that his hunch had been a good one. He picked up his carrying case and put a forceful hand on Charles G. Morton's elbow. "Inside, Tim. Got to straighten this out quietly."

Unwillingly the big man permitted himself to be shepherded through the door. Jeff Landry looked at Johnny and followed them inside. Johnny closed the door, and stood with his back against it.

"Now suppose you tell me—" Tim Connor began in the familiar shattering roar, then stopped as Johnny raised a hand.

"Jeff." Johnny's voice was quiet. "Mr. Morton's dog died." It was a statement.

Jeff looked surprised. "It was a cat, but it died, all right. I called his wife—"

"Poisoned," Johnny interrupted, again in the flat statement.

"Yes." Jeff paused. "You knew? How—"

"I didn't know, Jeff." Johnny moved away from the door, casually. "But Mr. Morton knew. Didn't you, Mr. Morton?"

"What's all this tomfoolery!" "Mr. Morton" glared from Johnny to Jeff and back again. He made up his mind suddenly and advanced on Johnny, the round face dark. "You sucked me in here, wise guy! I—"

The resonant voice died to a gasp as Johnny put a palm in the center of the cream-colored sport jacket and shoved firmly. Tim Connor staggered back on his heels a quick half-dozen steps, his arms flailing the air. Beside Johnny in the narrow corridor Jeff Landry took a quick step forward. "Is this the guy?" he demanded tensely. "Is he the one?"

"Easy, Jeff," Johnny counseled. He turned back to the big man. "You should have bought a program, Tim. You guessed wrong on the lineup; I'm in the other dugout."

Bitter anger mottled the moon face. "I won't forget this, Killain. I'll cure you of meddling. I'll drop a ton on you."

"That's for later. Right now let's clean house here."

"Right now I'm getting out of here!" Tim Connor fixed his panama more firmly with an impatient tug at the brim. "And God help the man who tries to stop me!"

At his first step Johnny moved fast; he crowded up against the beefy figure, and Tim Connor retreated the step as his right hand darted under the cream-colored jacket. Johnny pivoted on the ball of his left foot and muscle-punched the reaching right arm with a line-drive right-hand smash. The big man's face went white, and his arm dropped limply as his body caromed from the wall. He made no effort to resist as Johnny snaked the snub-nosed revolver from the shoulder sling under the sport coat and tossed it back to Jeff.

Johnny looked at Tim Connor's suddenly shriveled face

113

and at the left hand supporting the right arm. "You're gettin' old, Tim. You're about fifteen years and forty pounds away from gettin' out of here your way. You want to try mine?"

"I'll . . . get you for this, Killain—" The voice was still deep, but the vibrancy was gone. The heavy body was half crouched forward, but not aggressively; the face looked sick. "I'll . . . Let's hear your proposition."

"Conversation."

Tim Connor considered Johnny. "And?"

"If it reads you walk out of here."

"Just a damn minute!" Jeff Landry tried to push by the bar of Johnny's extended arm. "If this is the guy that poisoned those animals he's not going to walk out of here!"

"Listen to me, Jeff." Johnny said it quickly; he pushed the veterinarian back down the corridor and out of Tim Connor's hearing as he lowered his own voice. "You got a lot of money invested here, and you had a close call. We got a break and you're out of the barrel, but you go working this guy over he can tie you up indefinitely with assault charges and damage suits. Use your head."

"Those animals—" Jeff began stubbornly, and paused. He took a slow step backward. "Get him out of here, then. Fast. Before I change my mind."

Johnny walked back to Tim Connor. "Let's hear it, Tim."

The beefy man swallowed visibly. "Hear? What else is to hear? You laid it all out on the drawing board."

"I want to hear it from you, and right now. That's a soundproof door there, and Jeff is a little restless. Talk."

"If I do I walk out?"

"If I think I'm hearing it all."

"I was hired to scare Landry away from this address," Tim Connor said abruptly. "It figured that a little bad publicity ought to change his mind that his lease couldn't be bought up." He hesitated, and his eyes went warily to Jeff. He cleared his throat tentatively before continuing. "I sent two people in with dogs which had already been fed a pill set to dissolve in ten to twelve hours. This last time it was a cat." He hesitated again and shrugged. "That's it; somehow you caught it. I still don't see how—"

"Who hired you?" It was Jeff's voice; Jeff's glasses were in his pocket, and his tone was shrill.

114

Tim Connor replied promptly as he kept an uneasy eye on Jeff. "Man named Dave Richman."

Jeff looked at Johnny, who shook his head. "Never heard of him. It figures. This kind of thing filters down from five or six removes away from the operator like Connor here. With a lot of time and trouble and money you might be able to trace it back. You might. There's a better way."

"There's a way to do it right!" Jeff said it between his teeth, and then his shoulders slumped tiredly and he turned away. "All right; I said it before. Do it your way. Get him out of here."

Johnny nodded. "You heard the man, Tim. Get lost."

The big man needed no second invitation. With a careful eye on Jeff he sidled to the door and eased himself out into the waiting room. Johnny stepped into the doorway to make sure he kept on going, and he smiled at Jeff as he stepped back inside. "He hit just about three of the high spots on the way across the room."

"I shouldn't have let him get away with it," Jeff said leadenly. The fingers of the hand that traced the lean jawline trembled visibly. "Those helpless animals—"

"You did it right, Jeff. You were vulnerable. Still are, until you rivet this down. This is what you want to do—call up . . . Say, are you listening?"

"I'm listening. Go ahead."

"Call up your landlord and tell him to send this lawyer around, that you want to talk to him. But do it fast, before this gets back to him. He'll think you want to settle. When you get him in here, the first thing you do is bounce his tail a foot off the floor. Then you tell him about Tim Connor and Dave Richman like you had them stuffed in your hip pocket. Tell him they've blown the whistle on the whole racket. Tell him that the next thing that goes wrong around this place you're comin' after him and nail his ears to the nearest telephone pole. Can you do that?"

"My pleasure, believe me." Jeff drew a shallow breath. "How can I ever thank you, Johnny? I'm just beginning to realize I'm out from under this nightmare."

"You're not out till you muzzle this lawyer," Johnny pointed out. "If you don't make him think he's a hostage he's just going to try something else." He stooped to pick up the carrying case. "You know who you should really thank? White stuff here."

"The kitten?"

"It was a kitten Connor—or Morton—sent in, wasn't it?" Jeff's eyes widened. "A white Persian!"

"Sure. It was supposed to be this one. It came to me while I was listenin' to Connor bellow outside. I intercepted Sassy here one step short of her being turned over to Connor's partner. She was earmarked for here. When the delivery broke down they had to get a replacement."

Jeff Landry ran a finger lightly across the front of the wire mesh, and Sassy's pink nose followed it interestedly. "Eight lives left, little one. You don't look worried. Johnny, she has a gold lifetime pass around this place, and I hope she never needs it." He put out his hand, and Johnny took it.

"Glad it worked out, Jeff."

"So am I, Johnny. So am I."

On the street Johnny was surprised to find a light rain falling. He walked up to the corner and caught a west-bound cab just when he began to think he was going to have to start walking. In the cab he ran up the windows and took Sassy out of her carrying case. She seemed delighted to see him; she frisked around his feet on the floor and made several brisk, stinging sorties up his shins and thighs. He had difficulty getting her back in the case when they reached the hotel.

He walked down the alley and in through the subbasement entrance and rang for the service elevator. While waiting he removed his shirt and draped it over the black plastic case. When the elevator door opened Johnny got aboard, and Charlie, a wizened gnome with a facial tic who operated the service elevator on the middle shift, nodded grudgingly. He glanced at the shirt-covered case in Johnny's hand as the elevator started up. "What'cha got there, John?"

"King cobra. Take a look?"

"Pass. Knowin' you, it could be."

They rode in silence to the sixth floor, and in his own room Johnny unlatched the drop-down front of the case. Sassy crept out cautiously, took a long look around and with tail aloft and four white paws twinkling galloped to the re-frigerator, where she crouched expectantly. Johnny smiled, then remembered the diet list. He slapped his pockets experimentally, pulled it out and studied it. He glanced down at the vigilant kitten. "I got a feelin' you're not gonna approve of this, baby doll."

116

He took down two of Sassy's saucers and fixed one of milk and one of water. With one eye cocked sideways at him from above the newspaper he spread, Sassy took a dozen halfhearted laps at the milk, and then sat back on her haunches and looked at him reproachfully.

"The man says liquids for another twenty-four hours," Johnny apologized to her. "Then lean meat, and not too much of it."

The kitten wrinkled her nose at the proposal; when she saw that nothing else was to be forthcoming she returned to the milk. Johnny watched her for a moment, then stripped the bed. He kicked off his shoes and stretched out with a sigh. He tried to blank out his mind; he could use a little sleep.

On the floor below him Sassy came back into his line of vision, walking toward him with her short, mincing steps. With no visible effort she floated upward and landed on the bed beside him, settled down in the circle of his arm and curled herself up into a tight little ball. From the small body there came a deep, purring sound; Johnny lifted his head from the pillow to look down at her. "Shut off your motor, white stuff." He dropped back to the pillow—and oblivion.

The telephone jarred him awake; he grabbed at it. "Yeah?"

"Eleven-thirty, Johnny."

"Thanks, Edna." He yawned, stretched and rubbed his eyes. He had slept either too long or not long enough. He couldn't wake up. He sat up on the edge of the bed finally, then reluctantly propelled himself into the shower. The cold water helped; on the way down to the lobby he tried to recall when he had eaten last. His backbone and ribs felt too close together.

He walked on out through the foyer to the street; Forty-fifth Street's neon complement of lights glowed mistily in the rain that was now a steady downpour. He had a double order of ham and eggs and three cups of black coffee at the greasy spoon four doors up the street, and he felt almost awake when he returned to the lobby.

Marty Seiden waved at him from the front desk, and Johnny returned the wave and then pulled up short. He walked over to the desk, and Marty looked up at him expectantly. "I hear you got a letch for the blonde on the balcony, kid."

Marty's grin was sheepish. "It makes me unusual?"

117

"It puts you in bad company." Johnny studied the unease in the sharp features under the red hair. "I'll lay it on the line, Marty. You been puttin' out information on guests in the hotel to the blonde, for services rendered, maybe?" The boy tugged self-consciously at his bow tie. "Just put this in your peace pipe, kid—there's gonna be a big, loud noise up on that balcony shortly. Are you covered?"

Marty Seiden swallowed. "I will be. And thanks."

Johnny nodded, and turned away from the desk. At the bell captain's desk Paul was glumly studying the log. "Middle shift had only seven check-ins since six o'clock."

"Better'n we'll do, if this rain keeps up," Johnny predicted. "Damn these quiet nights, anyway. I can't stay awake. If you see Mike Larsen come in, Paul, tell him to see me before he goes upstairs."

He hadn't had a chance yet to check with Mike on the folder of carbons he had taken away from Mavis Delaroche. Mike would probably know whether it was more likely to be a part of Russo's over-all operation or whether the blonde was in business for herself unknown to Russo.

Paul tapped him on the arm. "Lend me your key to Chet's office. Marty needs transcript sheets."

"I'll run up myself. If I don't keep movin', I'll fall over sideways." Johnny dug out his keys, detoured to the switch box and turned out the main overhead lights in the lobby, and in the familiar gloom climbed the stairs to the mezzanine. There was a light on in the public stenographer's office which went out even as he looked, and the door opened. Ed Russo walked out of the office, accompanied by a tall blonde; for an instant Johnny thought it was Mavis, and then he saw that this woman was older. Attractive, if you liked the lean, greyhound type. She had the lacquered look of money.

On impulse Johnny stepped into the curtained circular lounge; he was not hidden if anyone looked in there, but he was not out in plain sight, either.

Ed Russo closed the door of his office and shifted a package under his arm as he fumbled for his key. "Take mine, Ed," the woman said. Her voice was low, but crisp. She removed a key from her bag and handed it to him. "Thanks for taking this trouble for me on such short notice."

"No trouble, Mrs. Sanders." Ed Russo tried the locked door and handed her back the key. "All part of the day's work.

118

I'm only sorry the other news tonight couldn't have been a little better." He led the way toward the stairs.

So this was the widow Sanders; Johnny craned to see better, but they were moving away from him. Johnny found it interesting that the widow Sanders not only was on a first name basis with Ed Russo, but actually had a key to his office.

When the descending heads on the stairs passed below floor level he went into action. He ran back across the mezzanine to Chet Rollins' office, opened it hurriedly, grabbed up a handful of transcript sheets and ran back downstairs to the lobby. He slapped the sheets down on the registration desk in front of Marty Seiden and sprinted out to the foyer. As he had hoped, Russo and the widow were still in sight, on the sidewalk under the marquee; as he looked the woman raised her umbrella, and the pair turned left and started toward Seventh Avenue.

Johnny shot into the checkroom behind the bell captain's desk and snatched a raincoat from a hook. From the looks of it it wouldn't shed much rain, but it would cover the uniform. Paul stepped off the nearer elevator as Johnny emerged from the checkroom, and he pointed to the raincoat. "Back in a few minutes, Paul."

He dashed out to the street and breathed more freely when he saw the umbrella two-thirds of the way toward the avenue. He hadn't lost them. He crossed the street at a trot and took up the chase from the other side, settling down to a long stride that gained rapidly for him.

The rain was a steady drizzle; it looked like being a damp pursuit. And then, as he drew closer to his quarry from a parallel position across the street, in an instant it changed from pursuit to decision. Across Seventh, at the corner of Forty-fifth and Broadway Russo handed the widow the package he had been carrying, and with no exchange at all that Johnny could see widow, package and umbrella turned north on Broadway while Ed Russo continued west on Forty-fifth.

Johnny hesitated and then decided for Russo. The sharp-featured man was on the street in the rain with no hat, raincoat or umbrella now, and he gave no indication of looking for a cab. Ed Russo increased Johnny's interest in the next fifty yards by turning left on Eighth Avenue where he walked the block to Forty-fourth and turned back east, so

119

that as Johnny once again took up the chase from the opposite side of the street the original direction had been reversed.

Between Eighth and Broadway Russo stepped into a doorway, but it was only to turn up the collar of his jacket. So it was not to be a short trip, then; Johnny settled down to it. He was more curious than ever now about Ed Russo's destination, since it appeared to be one that the man felt he had to walk to, in the rain. They crossed Seventh again, and the Avenue of the Americas and Fifth, and between Fifth and Madison Johnny made a discovery. He was not the only one following Russo. A man in an oilskin slicker stayed a steady two-thirds of a block behind the oblivious target.

This observation was confirmed almost at once when Russo turned left on Madison and the slicker followed. Johnny dropped back a little further; let the slicker follow Russo, and he would follow the slicker. Russo turned right again on Forty-sixth; he had evidently only wanted to by-pass the Grand Central building. The procession trekked damply across Park, Lexington and Third, and at Second Avenue Russo turned right again for two blocks to Forty-fourth, and at Forty-Fourth turned east again.

From the opposite side of Second Avenue Johnny made the long diagonal as he kept the oilskin slicker in sight. The slicker turned the corner of Forty-fourth, looked east and broke into a run. From the middle of Second Avenue Johnny accelerated through the puddles, and turned the corner himself.

On Forty-fourth Street Ed Russo was nowhere to be seen at all. The oilskin slicker was forty feet from the corner, poised doubtfully before two narrow alleys, practically side by side, that meandered off almost at right angles into the wet darkness. Evidently he hadn't seen which one Russo had taken.

The speed at which Johnny negotiated the corner caught the slicker's attention; he turned and stared. Rather than turn back and invite inquiry, Johnny walked on more sedately; he would have walked right on by, but the slicker stepped into his path and barred the way.

"I thought so!" the slicker said grimly. "There couldn't be two that big out on a night like this."

Johnny stared down into the wet, angry features of Detective James Rogers and for once in his life was at a loss for words.

"Well?" Jimmy Rogers demanded. "I'm listening. What—"

His staccato inquiry choked. In the darkness and rain an automatic pistol went off four times, soggy sounds in the soggy night.

"He's got someone else!" Johnny said tightly.

Detective Rogers said nothing at all; he turned and ran up the nearer alley, and Johnny ran hard at his heels.

CHAPTER 12

HE SLOGGED HEAVILY OVER THE UNEVEN cobblestoned footing up the close-walled alleyway between the dark warehouses, a step and a half behind the bobbing flashlight in the hand of Jimmy Rogers. They burst into a wider areaway with a slight downgrade; the rapid circular movement of the flashlight disclosed cement loading platforms on three sides of the rough inner square. The alley was a dead end.

Johnny stood on tiptoe as the flash returned to its starting point and made a slow, probing semicircle of the loading area, picking up the blank-faced, whitewashed doors and the dusty concrete freight-handling surfaces which the steady rain had turned to pasty mud at their unprotected outer edges.

He pushed up behind the slender, intent detective. "You think we come up the wrong alley?"

The sandy-haired man made no reply. He started the light on another tour of the darkness, this time at ground level. Two-thirds of the way around the circuit Johnny grunted as the bright beam wavered and then locked down on a shapeless bundle prone in the shallow puddles of the pitted roadbed of the alley.

"Jackpot," Detective Rogers said tersely and trotted to the still figure. At his shoulder Johnny looked down unbelievingly at the white face and staring eyes and the head with most of its top gone. Ed Russo lay dead in the wet night, the nearest puddle stained a bright red, and Johnny mentally rocked back on his heels.

The detective knelt and felt for a pulse, although the condition of the head made it only a formality. He straightened, fished a handkerchief out from under the slicker, and wiped off his hands. "Kaput," he said unnecessarily. His light left the body to make another swing around the cement loading platforms. "—nine, ten, eleven," he counted. His voice was bitter. "Eleven warehouse doors leading off this rabbit warren, and our man needed a key to only one. What a spot for an ambush." The light returned to the body. "Looks like he got it at eye level. Then fell—or was pushed—down here."

Johnny had trouble finding his voice. "How wrong can you get? I thought this guy was pitchin', not catchin'. This stones me. When we heard the shots out on the street I figured for sure he'd scratched someone else breathin' on his neck."

"Where'd you pick him up?"

"At the hotel. He was with the widow over there. I didn't make you until between Fifth and Madison coming east."

"I saw the widow. We'll talk to her." Detective Rogers wiped a trickle of rain from his face and amended his statement. "Or somebody will. This one's out of our territory— first one not in the precinct. Walk out to the corner and see if you can locate the beat man. If not, call in. Not our place; it's not our baby. Yet."

"You want me back here?"

"Certainly I want you back here. The local boys will have a few hundred assorted questions for you. Lucky for you I was standing right beside you when we heard those shots. That about used up your luck, though, because when the lieutenant finds out you were seventy-five yards away when Russo got it, you bought a tough ticket. You know what he told you."

"He told me to stay away from the people in the public relations office. He didn't say a word about Russo."

"Correction. He said stay away from anyone connected with the case. You didn't consider it significant that the woman you saw Russo with before you took out after him now happens to own that public relations business?"

Johnny was silent, and Rogers looked him up and down. "You're heading for a fall, Johnny. You can't buck—"

"Ahhh, stow it!" Johnny interrupted angrily. "You people think you got a patent on me? You're beginning to sound just like all the rest."

"I have a job to do, and I do it the way I'm told," Detective Rogers said after a short pause; there was an edge in his voice. He stopped and slapped disgustedly at the wet leg of his trousers. "Forget it. I'm worse than you are for arguing with a mulehead like you. Go on out and get somebody in here. I'm an incipient pneumonia case right this minute."

Johnny headed out into the darkness and stumbled and splashed his way up the slight upgrade. It was black in the alley; he welcomed the comparative brightness of Forty-fourth Street. He stamped his feet on the sidewalk to remove the clinging mud which had oozed above the welt of his shoes. At the southeast corner of Second Avenue a broad-backed black raincoat glistened in the lights of the little all-night restaurant across the street, and Johnny walked up to the corner resignedly and tapped the raincoat on the arm. It turned, and elderly sharp blue eyes in a wide, pug-nosed face inspected Johnny carefully.

"Dead man in an alley up the street," Johnny told him. "There's a detective there now, and he'd like a little help."

"You know the detective's name, son?"

"Rogers."

There was slight movement beneath the raincoat. "No detective named Rogers in this precinct, son."

"He's from West Fifty-fourth."

The patrolman grunted. "I hear you saying so. What happened to the guy in the alley?"

"He lost the top of his head."

The wide mouth pursed doubtfully. "I ought to take a look first. Still, you don't look like the jack-rabbit type. Mind you, if I turn the precinct out on a night like this, and there's nothing in that alley, I'll knock your ears down."

"Go ahead and make your call," Johnny said impatiently.

The big shoulders hitched at the raincoat. "You come right along with me, son, and watch me make it. I want my eye on you."

Johnny half restrained a smile as he followed the patrolman across the street to the restaurant. From the bulge under the raincoat he knew that the service revolver had been unholstered; the officer was carrying it in his left hand,

and this created a problem for him when faced with the wall pay phone.

"Like me to dial for you?" Johnny offered. "Or I'll hold the gun."

The blue eyes inspected him critically for a moment, and then with a rustling of rubber the bulge disappeared. "Now I've got you in the light, son, you don't look quite like I made you on the street. Better get that nose straightened, though, before you apply to teach at Sunday school." He turned back to the wall phone, and dialed. "Glidden, Sergeant. Man reported . . ."

The patrolman's voice droned on while Johnny listened with just a fraction of his attention. Russo's death had collapsed completely the major props of the framework within which he had been working. Somewhere, now, there was a man who had committed four murders, and he hadn't the slightest notion who it was.

He wondered if the police were any closer. Would Jimmy Rogers have been tailing Russo if he expected any such blowoff as this tonight? It figured that Rogers had been just as wrong as he was.

Officer Glidden nodded to Johnny as he backed away from the telephone, and they walked back out into the rain. Johnny gingerly moved his shoulders beneath the raincoat, which had now become a blotter and passed on its absorption to the sodden uniform beneath. He couldn't remember the last time he had felt so uncomfortably wet.

Detective Rogers moved out from a dry corner of a warehouse platform as Officer Glidden's flashlight announced them from the alley. After a brief, low-voiced colloquy with the detective the big policeman laboriously removed a notebook from his raingear, folded it back ' painstakingly, heaved a mighty sigh and began writing. Johnny surmised that from Glidden's perfunctory questioning of him that Detective Rogers must have mentioned Johnny's actually being in his presence when the shots were heard. He didn't fool himself that the precinct detectives would be as easily satisfied; it looked like the beginning of a long night. When Glidden snapped his notebook shut with a grunt of relief Johnny spoke up with no real hope. "That wind me up, Chief? I could use some dry clothes."

"That's not for me to say, son." The patrolman looked around for Jimmy Rogers, then out at the mouth of the alley as headlights beamed through the narrow passageway into the semicircular dead end. The high beam of the car lights brilliantly illuminated the sprawled figure lying in the mud at the base of the loading area, and in the glare the rain beat down steadily. Other cars stacked up behind the first one and disgorged dark figures who moved purposefully; it was the type of night when a minimum of facts speedily arrived at was the goal of all concerned.

Johnny watched Patrolman Glidden jump heavily from the platform to the alley bed and advanced to meet the second contingent. His own position on the platform was not within the perimeter of the headlights, and he looked down for a moment at the activity in the arena of light below him. Take off, Killain, he told himself suddenly. Nobody's paying any attention to you. So they'll yank you in when they miss you later; they'll have to come and get you to do it, and at least you'll be dry.

He eased over to the darkest corner of the platform and jumped lightly to the mud below. He edged around the outer rim of the platforms and squeezed his way past the first of the parked cars. He had to brush past several latecomers on their way in from the street and he received several sharp glances, but no one offered to stop him. He walked swiftly away from the flashing red lights at the alley entrance and picked up a cab at the stand at the Second Avenue inter-section. He settled into the back seat and listened to the soggy squish; he oozed water from every stitch.

As the cab swung west he realized suddenly they were within a block or two of Vic's apartment, and he leaned forward. "Cut over south a block, Mac."

The cabbie turned left and looked over his shoulder when they came to the first corner. "Straight ahead?"

"One more block, anyway." He looked for a familiar land-mark as the cab rolled through the quiet streets. "Yeah. Turn right here." When the cab straightened out from the turn they were passing the apartment, and Johnny looked up at the second floor and saw the light on in the front room. He slapped the leather-covered back of the front seat sharply to attract the driver's attention. "Pull in here a minute."

"Listen, bud," the cabbie said disgustedly as the cab slowed and turned into the curb. "This is no night to be cruisin' on instruments. Make up your—"

"Shut up, will you?" Johnny thought it over. After three

now, and Lorraine was still up? Or she could have fallen asleep with the light on. It was hardly the hour for a social call—or was it? He opened the cab door and got out on the sidewalk. "What's the tab, Mac?"

"Thirty-five," the cabby said morosely and then brightened. "Say, thanks, Jack."

He walked past the familiar iron fence with its blunted pikes; he thought back fleetingly to that merry-go-round he had stumbled into coming out of this apartment. One more thing that had never been explained satisfactorily. With the aid of his cigarette lighter he found the right buzzer, and Lorraine's voice came so quickly he knew she could not have been asleep.

"Yes? Who is it?"

"Johnny."

A faint murmur of sound. Surprise? "Come up."

He climbed the stairs; she was in the apartment door in pajamas and dressing gown, both of a lightish blue color that did nothing for the dark circles under her eyes. She looked tired, and her hair was disheveled and damp-looking. She closed the door behind him and patted at her hair defensively when she caught him looking at it. "It's a mess, I know; I'm just out of the shower, and I need to set it." She looked at his wet clothing. "What have you been up to on a night like this?"

He didn't answer her. He took another hard look at her hair and deliberately pushed his way past her into the bathroom. The light was on, but the tub was dry. So was the shower stall; so were the neatly folded towels. He opened the hamper; no wet towels. He turned to find her in the doorway, and he could see the storm clouds in her face as he accused her. "You've been out in the rain, that's why your hair's wet. You just got in ahead of me."

The voice was mocking, but there was an edge to it. "You've heard of a shampoo, no doubt?"

"First it was a shower." So it was important to her to deny that she had been out tonight? He brushed her out of the doorway as she stood in his way, and bright anger flared in her face; back in the front hall he opened the closet door and ran a probing hand down the line of hanging clothing. It was not hard to find; his questing fingers picked up the wet folds of a raincoat, and he took it down from the rod,

126

hanger and all, and flourished it at her. "You shampoo this, too?"

"Put that back where you found it." Her voice was hard.

"When I get good an' ready I'll put it back, Lorraine." He turned the raincoat in his hands; beneath it he could feel other clothing on the hanger. He peeled back the wet rubber and looked down at a black-and-white checked jacket and a pair of gray flannel slacks wet from the knees down. He stared at their wrinkled dampness for a moment before he turned back to the woman. "Let's hear something," he demanded grimly.

Two bright spots blazed in the pale cheeks; Lorraine Barnes had not lost her poise, but the same could not be said for her temper. She was furious. "I'll let you hear something. You get out of here, this minute, and you stay out. I'll thank you to mind your own business. Now get out!"

He shoved the jacket and slacks at her. "Don't you think you should have burned these after you killed Roberta Perry?"

"Burned—" She looked suddenly uncertain of herself. He could see her almost repeating aloud the description of the clothing seen on the man on Roberta Perry's fire escape. Man? A short, stocky man . . . or a tall, plump woman? She looked at the jacket and slacks in his hand as though she were seeing them for the first time. "That's not . . . those aren't— It's simply a . . . coincidence—" Her voice trailed off; he could see that she was thinking hard, but she recovered quickly. "I'll still thank you—"

She broke off as he dropped the wet garments on the floor and took her by the arms, not gently. "I'm through foolin' around," he said between his teeth. "Where were you tonight?"

She tried to twist away. "Let go of me!" Her face was scarlet. "Let go!"

He held her effortlessly. "Where were you? I'm sick of this one-way deal. You'll tell me if I have to raise lumps all over you."

"If you think—you can third degree me. . . . I'll show you —different!" she panted breathlessly, and with a surge of anger he picked her up by the shoulders and in four long strides carried her inside to the sofa, where he dropped her. She bounced high and landed asprawl with head snapped back. The blue-gray eyes stared up at him malevolently as he pulled up a chair in front of her and seated himself, hemming her in. He made his voice deliberate. "Make it easy on yourself, Lorraine. Fast or slow, you're going to talk. I played along with you all I'm goin' to. From right here we do it my way."

Her lips were drawn back from her teeth; there was no fear in her. "Let me remind you, Johnny—because I have a stake in this myself I refuse to be caught in the down-draft of your emotional involvement. That's final. Now get up out of that chair."

"You're not talkin' to your husband Vic's friend, Lorraine. You're talkin' to Johnny Killain, who used to be married to Ellen Saxon, an' I want answers. What's the matter? Don't you have an alibi for Russo tonight?"

"Russo? Alibi? What's—" Her teeth gnawed at her lower lip, and she sat up straighter on the sofa. The anger vanished from her face as though with a sponge. "What happened tonight, Johnny? You've got to tell me."

"Lady, you've got more brass than a foundry. I've got to tell you, have I? Those days are gone. I gave you a chance to join the team an' you turned me down." His mind veered off on a tangent; he leaned back and considered her carefully. "Did Ed Russo work for Robert Sanders?" he asked her abruptly.

She looked surprised. "I've already told you that it was Mrs. Sanders he worked for over there."

"But if it was out of the same office—"

She shook her head. "The public relations business doesn't work like that," she said patiently. "They each had their own clients and their own staff." She tried to make her voice placating. "What's all this about Russo? What happened tonight, Johnny?"

"We're gettin' off the subject. Where were you tonight? I want to know. Now."

The red spots were back in her face, but her tone was restrained in her effort to appear casual. "If you think you can find out anything from me I don't want you to know, then you just don't know me very well."

He leaned toward her. "Where were you tonight, Lorraine?"

Her eyes narrowed. "If you're not on your way out that door in five seconds I'll rip these pajamas and start screaming."

"Suit yourself. You won't be screamin' when they get here."

128

Her short upper lip curled. "You frighten me. Terribly. I'm speechless with fear." But she made no move toward the pajamas; she spoke again quickly. "Don't let's do this to each other, Johnny. I have the best of reasons for everything I've done. I *have* to do it my way."

"Not any more. Cut the stalling. Talk!"

"Find out, then, you fool!" she gritted and, in movement nearly too quick to follow, braced her back against the sofa, drew up her knees tightly to her chest and as part of the same motion straightened them viciously, exploding her slippered heels with projectile force against Johnny's breastbone as he leaned forward in his chair. The impact was tremendous; only his weight prevented the chair from going over backward, and he teetered uncertainly in mid-air for an instant before he could rock himself level again.

She stared up at him unbelievingly as he fought against the knifelike assault on his lungs; when he stumbled erect and kicked the chair behind him fear washed her face a pasty gray. She lurched up and tried to duck past him as he stood bent nearly double, and he half straightened with an effort and slapped her heavily. She gasped and fell back on the sofa, the mark of his hand standing in livid relief on her cheek.

Fear and anger struggled for dominance in her distorted face as she stared up at him, and the livid finger marks turned a dull red. When Johnny could speak at all his voice was a croak. "Not a bad move for a hundred-twenty-five-pound female woman. Too bad you didn't know I was comin'. You coulda had your high heels on, then, an' hung your spikes in me."

"Don't think I wouldn't!"

"I think you would. How many people you decommissioned with that move? Four inches lower you had a perfect gut shot; six inches higher you break my neck. I could see you were surprised I didn't go over; you got a real bad break, huh? You learn that one in finishin' school?"

"Oh, stop it!" Weariness had replaced the fear, but there was still no color in her face except for the mark of his hand. "I should have known better than to try to knock over a chunk of pig iron like you. You got me mad, that's all. I'm sorry."

"Skip the sorry. Talk."

The tip of her tongue circled her lips swiftly; she appeared

129

to be gauging his mood. "I suppose you feel you have all the justification you need now to beat it out of me. That should make you feel good. That should—"

"Will you stop the stalling?" Johnny's voice cut across hers, hard. "Talk!"

And as though the explosive imperative had been a signal the apartment buzzer sounded in the hallway. Lorraine looked surprised but started to rise; he made one halfhearted move to stop her and then shrugged. He knew who it was. It just wasn't his night.

"Who?" Lorraine asked the speaker. "Oh." She hesitated and half turned to look at Johnny in the doorway. "Well . . . come on up." She scooped up her wet raincoat, jacket and slacks from the floor where Johnny had dropped them and threw them into a corner of the hall closet. She stood with her back pressed against the closet door and looked at him speculatively. "It's Cuneo. I'm not fussy about his finding you here this time of night. On the other hand, I'm not fussy about being left alone with you here, either." She frowned as she moved away from the door. "Why is he here?"

"Whyn't you ask him?"

"But I need to know—" She chewed at her lip in the familiar gesture. "We can still work together, Johnny," she said persuasively.

"Not a chance. A clean divorce."

"Just a minute!" she called to the knock at the door. She turned back to Johnny with the first hint of desperation in her tone. "You can't do this to me now! I need to know what happened!"

"Open the door," he said inexorably. "You're doin' all right. You're still walkin' around, and there's four people that aren't."

Her eyes widened. "Four!"

"Open the door."

She opened it, reluctantly. Ted Cuneo stalked in, hesitated at sight of her nightwear, sensed the other presence and whirled to look at Johnny. "Well, for— What are you doing here, Killain?"

"Do I need a license from you to be here?"

The detective turned to stare at Lorraine. "You two—" he said slowly. He looked at her more closely. "What's the matter with your face?"

In the split second that she hesitated Johnny could see that

130

she was wondering if she could somehow involve him with Cuneo without involving herself. With evident regret she decided against it. "Nothing that a little cold water won't fix. I believe I took the decision on points."

Detective Cuneo seemed to swell. "You mean he hit you, Mrs. Barnes?"

"Not often enough," Johnny said harshly, and Lorraine Barnes laughed almost gaily.

"Johnny and I never understood one another better. He was just leaving."

"Right now," Johnny agreed. He turned experimentally to the door. If Cuneo knew about his unheralded departure from Second Avenue . . .

Cuneo didn't, evidently. "Anyone talked to you tonight?" he asked Johnny sharply, his side glance at Lorraine indicating that he didn't want to say too much.

"Yeah," Johnny said laconically. "I was with Rogers."

"You were with—" The large-pupilled eyes swung back to Lorraine and caught her hard, interrogating stare. He gestured dismissingly. "I'll talk to you later, Killain."

"Sure you will," Johnny agreed softly. He smiled at Lorraine, then walked out of the apartment and down the stairs out into the still dripping night.

CHAPTER 13

IN THE RAINSWEPT, DESERTED STREET Johnny scowlingly squished along back toward the hotel; not a cab in sight, naturally. A little more water might be just what you need, Killain . . . reduce a little of the steam coming out of your thick ears after that fiasco upstairs. Damn that Lorraine woman, anyway. . . . Damn all women eating their cake and trying to have it, too—

He came to a dead stop in the middle of the block.

Women . . .

There's a woman on the fringe of this deal at whom you haven't taken a very close look, friend. Quite a considerable woman—name of Mavis Delaroche. You think maybe she was out in the rain tonight, too? You think you could get her to tell you why, if she were? Mavis. You've never gotten the answer yet on those one-copy carbons of hers, either.

He hunched his shoulders under the sodden raincoat and propelled himself forward again. He grunted impatiently as he stepped down off the curb into a puddle of water; across the street he turned right and headed for the lights of the all-night drugstore two blocks over. At its entrance he wrung a little of the surplus water from himself and marched inside to the phone booth. He dialed the hotel and removed his handkerchief from his pocket and placed it lightly before his lips. "Front desk," he said mufflledly.

He waited for the click of Sally's cut-off key before answering Marty Seiden's "Front desk, Seiden."

"Don't let on, Marty; this is Johnny. Call me 'sir'."

"Right you are, sir."

"That big blonde up on the balcony . . . what's her address? An' don't mention her name."

"Address?" He could hear the surprise in the red-haired night clerk's voice. "Uh—332 East 63rd."

"You payin' the rent up there?"

"In that neighborhood? I couldn't pay her maid service. You're outta your mind. Sir." Marty's tone was injured.

"Okay. Tell Paul I'll be hung up a little while yet."

He left the booth and ran an appraising eye up and down the half-dozen assorted coffee drinkers at the counter. "Any of you guys hackin'?"

A cup clattered into its saucer, and a gray-haired man in horn-rimmed spectacles stood up immediately. "That's me, boss. Where to?"

"Let's go," Johnny said noncommittally and led the way outside. Never tell your business to a roomful of listening ears . . . well, okay, but are you ever going to relax a little bit from the ingrained caution of the old days? he asked himself impatiently. Who do you think gives a damn about you, or what you're up to now?

In the cab he gave the uptown address and settled back for the ride. You've still got a problem, Killain . . . in that neighborhood you're nine-to-five not to even get inside the front door. If there isn't a doorman there'll be a night switchboard operator, plus probably an elevator operator, all of them likely to be a little crusty over a tenant being disturbed at four A.M.

He paid off the cab in front of the towering apartment building and stood on the curb until it pulled away. Automatically he fumbled up the collar of the raincoat, though there wasn't a dry quarter of an inch on it, and crossed the street to reconnoiter a little less conspicuously. He stood on the opposite sidewalk in the blowing rain and looked up at the acres of windows with only an occasional light behind them.

No doorman visible—fine. Unless the old boy was inside sneaking a smoke, or dodging the rain. Through the front entrance he could see the closed elevator doors, and even as he looked they opened and a uniformed figure emerged and turned left. Johnny hastily skipped a damp fifteen feet to his right to keep the uniform in sight and watched it settle down lackadaisically behind a small counter that could only be a lobby switchboard.

You must be getting lucky, Killain . . . no doorman, and the switchboard operator is also the elevator operator. He can't be in two places at once. Remind yourself to send that economy-minded building superintendent a carton of cigarettes tomorrow.

He waited twenty increasingly wet minutes for the elevator doors to close again, and when the uniformed figure disappeared behind them, Johnny crossed the street at a shambling trot. In the foyer he quickly picked out Delaroche on the mailboxes—3-C—and entered the lobby. The only sign of life was the wavering trail of smoke from the unattended cigarette in the ashtray by the switchboard, and he headed quickly for the stairs.

From the third floor landing he padded silently down the lushly carpeted hallway and stopped in front of 3-C. He listened an instant, and then pushed the ivory bell button. Inside he could hear a faint chime; he waited fifteen seconds and pressed it again. He thought he could hear faint movement from behind the door; he counted to ten and rang again.

"Who is it?"

He could barely hear the voice; he raised his own. "The iceman."

"The ice—" The door opened three inches on a chain latch, and Mavis' sleep-filled features under the tousled blonde hair

133

peered out suspiciously. "You! What the hell do you want?"

"That's an easy one, dimples. I want in."

She sniffed loudly. "On your way, buster. On your—"

"Look, kid," he interrupted her softly. "It just so happens I don't care what kind of noise I make out here getting in. How about you?"

She stared out at him malevolently. "Did Sam bring you up here without calling me?"

"Sam has yet to see me. If there's a beef, Sam's likely to accuse you of aiding and abetting."

She hesitated another instant, and then with a soft rattle of the chain the door opened and Johnny slipped inside. He took a quick look around the comfortably furnished bed-sitting room, softly illuminated by the bedside lamp, and turned to include Mavis' king-sized pajama-clad figure in his approving inspection. "You fit those pajamas good, kid. Real good."

The small mouth pursed sulkily. "Why I ever let you in . . . You're nothing but trouble—"

He paid no attention to her. "That a closet?" He gestured at a closed door.

"That's the bathroom. What—"

"This must be the closet, then," he deduced, stepped forward and opened the door. He ran his hand sweepingly down the racks of clothing and backed out thoughtfully. Dry— all dry. He didn't know if he were disappointed or not.

Mavis emerged from her open-mouthed surprise, advanced and pushed him solidly. She did a double take when nothing happened at the push, but her voice came more strongly. "What the hell's going on here, you big moose?"

Johnny looked at her admiringly—no violet, Mavis. "What's the matter, small fry?" he asked her. "Am I supposed to bank into the side pocket like your boy friends when you lean on 'em?" He swung himself out of the dripping raincoat. "I need a shower."

"Sh-shower?" The big girl's voice was a strangled squeak as Johnny rapidly skinned himself out of his saturated uniform, tie, shirt and underwear.

"Get me something dry I can get into," he told her and bent to remove shoes and socks before walking into the bathroom.

She followed him to the door, eyes popping. "You crazy?" she hissed at him. "You one of those damn narcis . . .

134

narciss—" She gave it up. "You get the hell out! You try-ing to get me thrown out of here? This is a respectable place!"

"You want me to catch cold?" he asked reasonably, then turned on the shower and ducked inside. Above the rush-ing sound of the steaming hot water he could hear Mavis fuming, but when he emerged and groped for a towel a pair of tan slacks and a rose-colored sweater lay on the toilet seat. He dried himself roughly and slipped on the slacks; the two top buttons refused to meet over his lean middle. He picked up the sweater, looked at it and shook his head disgustedly. Barefooted he carried it out and waved it at Mavis where she sat in an armchair with a half-consumed cigarette in her hand. She looked up at his entrance, looked away and then back again as though fascinated. He noticed that she had combed her hair. "You dressin' Singer's midgets? I couldn't get one arm in this thing, an' I got about a leg an' a half in these pants. What else 've you got I can get decent in?"

"Nothing else!" she said spiritedly. "You must think this is a department store for elephants. You gone loco com-pletely, bustin' in on me like this?"

"I like you, kid. I don't give my business to just anyone." He slung the discarded sweater into an empty chair and casually approached the big girl. Before she realized his in-tention he loomed up over her chair, took her by the arms and lifted her out effortlessly, then carried her over to the bed where he sat down with her in his lap. Instinctively she fought against the pinioning arms, and for a moment he concentrated upon the exact amount of strength necessary to hold her immobile without hurting her. When she stopped struggling he relaxed his hold on her. "I told you, little one. I like you."

"One of us—is crazy!" she gasped. "You let me . . . up out of here!"

"I kind of like this arrangement. By the way, you never did get to tell me—that carbons bit your own idea?"

She twisted sharply until she could see his face. "Why do you want to know?"

He shrugged elaborately. "Maybe I could use a bright little girl in my business."

"You haven't any business," she said tartly, and then her tone softened. "You know you're the first soul in this world to call me 'little girl' since I was a kid? 'Course compared

135

to you . . . You're the biggest damn thing I ever—" Her voice trailed off.

"The carbons," Johnny repeated and pinched her.

She yipped and bucked in his lap. "Cut that out!"

He pinched her again, solidly.

"*Oww!* That *hurt*, damn you! I'll—" She flinched at the movement of his arm. "All right, all right, I'll tell you!" she said hastily. He waited, and she continued poutingly. "So it was my own idea. A girl's got to eat."

"A girl's got to keep her fantail outta the grease, too. You think Russo would front for you if someone caught you like I did?"

"I can handle Ed," she said confidently.

So she doesn't know about Ed, he thought. And she hasn't been out in the rain. Which about winds up the charade here. He looked at the big girl in his lap. Almost . . .

She was looking at him curiously. "Why? What's it to you?"

"Ask me tomorrow, kid." He upended her suddenly and dumped her sprawling across the rumpled bed; in an instant he was full-length beside her. "Funny thing," he said casually and fingered her pajamas. "These things nylon?" She nodded. "Thought so. I'm allergic to it. Just makes me want to pinch—" She kicked quickly at the advancing hand; he trapped the slim ankle in his left hand and rolled her onto her stomach. The big right hand dropped on the waistband of the pajamas. " 'Course it's only nylon makes me feel that way," he said thoughtfully and unhurriedly disposed of it. "Say now . . . that's nothing but fine. Real sugar-cured."

The big girl flipflopped like a grassed fish. "Put out that damn light!" she husked breathlessly.

"You think I'm an owl? Now you take this useful-lookin' appliance . . . you tested the horsepower lately?"

"Stop—it!"

Beside them he could see on the wall the magnified shadows blend suddenly as he bent over her purposefully. "You remind me, kid. Later."

136

CHAPTER 14

H<small>E WOKE IN THE LATE AFTERNOON</small> with a pain in his chest; he opened his eyes to find Sassy ensconced on her favorite spot. He lifted her off, and she swished her tail indignantly. "For somethin' that weighs about seven-eighths of a pound, white stuff, you sure walk like a Mack truck."

He picked up his wrist watch from the table and looked at it. He shook his head; he had been asleep for only an hour and a half. He had had nearly an all-day session with the police; they had landed in force shortly after his own return to the hotel, and only Jimmy Rogers' presence beside him at the critical moment and Patrolman Gliddens' admission that Johnny had not been specifically told to stay put prevented the occasion from being even stickier. The police were mad.

He lay back on the bed and explored with his hands the two dark spots just below his breastbone, so tender to the touch that the digging of the kitten's paws had awakened him. The twin souvenir of his early-morning encounter with Lorraine Barnes' heels had not only discolored but had swollen slightly. A fraction higher or lower, and she would really have sanded his engine.

Lorraine Barnes—now there was an all-purpose woman for you. Killed a husband of her own, according to Mike Larsen. Definitely not the delicate type in the clinches, yet with a distinct feminine appeal. Insistent upon doing her own snooping around four murders. And that savatte kick—where could she have learned that?

He stirred restlessly, leaned up on an elbow and reached for a cigarette from the pack on the table. He sucked in on the smoke and exhaled noisily as he lay down again. Sooner or later, Killain, he briefed himself, you're going to have to make up your mind about Lorraine Barnes. She may be Vic's wife, but the more you look at it she's about the only qualified entrant left in this murder derby, and the record says she's capable of it.

A motive? That was a little tougher. If Robert Sanders had been reneging on a romantic attachment she could have wanted him hung out to dry. She had a lot of pride. But the police seemed to have done nothing with that angle, which only went to show their sources of information might not be as good as Mike Larsen's. So—Sanders, possibly. But Ellen, and the Perry girl, and Russo? He felt that Lorraine Barnes was capable of very nearly anything in the white heat of anger, but the cold-blooded elimination of three more people—even though it could hardly have been planned that way originally—had a calculated touch to it that seemed foreign to her.

Still, on opportunity she rated high. By her own admission she had been close to Robert Sanders when he was killed. No one knew where she had been when Ellen Saxon was killed. She had not been at her apartment—or anywhere else that could be accounted for—when Roberta Perry was killed. And there were those clothes, so closely matching the description of the things worn by the killer. She had been out in the rain last night when Ed Russo caught the black pills. Four murders—and she had an alibi for none of them. But did you always have an alibi when you needed one, especially living alone?

He sat up on the edge of the bed. Well, boy, you've thought yourself full circle. Did she or didn't she? You're not likely to find out from her; you made hardly a dent in her head-on. Although if Cuneo hadn't shown—

He circled his drawn-up knees with his arms. Robert Sanders, Ellen Saxon, Roberta Perry, Ed Russo. Every one of them connected in one way or another with that public relations office. Some of them connected personally apparently not at all. That public relations office . . . Johnny stared thoughtfully at the far wall. Have you been missing a bet, Killain? There's at least one other person closely connected with the tight little group of deceased. The widow Sanders. Yet the police seemed to have no interest in her at all; her alibis must have been sheet steel.

Her husband and three of her employees. She'd been with Ed Russo last night just before he died. The widow Sanders . . .

He slid from the bed and reached for his clothes. He

thought of Lieutenant Dameron and shrugged. Cross that bridge when you come to it, Killain. The back of your hand to Joe Dameron, anyway.

He walked to the window and drew back the shade for a look outside. A little hazy. He closed the window against the chance of more rain. In the phone book he looked up the agency address and headed for the street. In the cab on the way over he tried to decide on an approach that would get him in to see the widow Sanders. He discarded two or three notions and finally gave it up; he'd think of something when the time came.

The agency offices were impressive; he looked around at the walnut paneling and the limed oak desk in the reception-ist's corner behind the little wooden fence before he spoke to the girl seated at the desk. "My name's Killain, and I'd like to see Mrs. Sanders. If she's busy I'll wait."

He had waited only five minutes when the girl beckoned to him. "Through that door and the third door on the right, sir."

The third door on the right was frosted all the way to the top and was completely unmarked. He knocked once and turned the knob. The tall blonde he had seen on the mez-zanine with Ed Russo last night sat behind a desk over-flowing with papers and half-filled ash trays. His first really good look at her disclosed clear, tanned skin and a healthy outdoors look, a little surprising in the executive type. Her linen suit stayed crisp-looking, even in the heat. The eyes were blue and direct; the mouth was firm, with a shade too much chin below it for prettiness. It was a strong face, and she did not boggle at his inspection.

"Mrs. Sanders, my name's Killain," Johnny said. He took a deep breath and waited for the next line to appear on the prompter's card.

"Helen Sanders," the tall woman amended absently. The blue eyes took him in inch by inch. "Killain. I don't seem to know the name, but don't I know— Of course; you're from the hotel." She smiled, a frank, open smile. "And you came to see me. That's rather remarkable, since I had already told someone to see you in the morning."

"See me, ma'am?"

"Exactly." The blue eyes retraced him, this time in quar-ter inches. "You've been at the hotel ten years, give or take a few months. I'm told that you exercise authority over and above what might reasonably be asked of you and ex-

139

ercise it well. Did you ever think of making a change?"

"What kind of a change, ma'am?"

"Mr. Killain—"

"The name is Johnny, ma'am," he interrupted her.

"Johnny, then. You'll forgive me, I hope, if I'm a little abrupt." Again the frank smile. "It's a habit of mine. I'm a businesswoman, not a sentimentalist. Ed Russo told me about you, and I checked you with another source. The public stenographer's office at the hotel is mine, Johnny. My money supported it, and Ed Russo ran it for me. I need a man to take Ed Russo's place, a man with a little raw intelligence, nerve and drive. Would you like to be that man?"

Johnny removed his cigarettes from his shirt pocket, shook one free and placed it in his mouth. As an afterthought he rose and offered one to the woman behind the desk; she accepted, and he lighted it for her. He sat down again and tried to keep his voice noncommittal. "I'd have thought Russo's attitude toward me might be a little negative."

Helen Sanders smiled again. "It was. So was the attitude of the other party I checked. I was told—even warned—not to make this offer to you." The smile widened; she had a really nice smile, Johnny decided. "I felt I had to decide for myself. The right man over there is worth a good deal to me, the wrong man is worthless."

"Does Tim Connor fit into the picture over there, Mrs. Sanders?"

"You've met Tim? I'll put it this way—Tim Connor was an independent contractor taken on by Ed for specific jobs. I personally feel that Connor was one of Ed's major mistakes."

"And here I thought Connor was a wheel."

"In his own circles, possibly; I can tell you explicitly that as far as the operation over there was concerned, far from being a wheel, Tim Connor was a very small gear."

Johnny settled back in his chair. "So you've warmed me up. Roll the cameras."

"Fair enough. The public stenographer bit is a blind, of course. The main purpose of that office is to serve as a briefing center for the people assigned to the special jobs which come out of my office here." Helen Sanders looked down momentarily at the glowing tip of her cigarette. "The girl there now will have to go, incidentally. I made it a practice not to interfere with Ed's pets, but she attracts entirely too much attention."

140

"You still haven't said anything," Johnny pointed out when she paused.

The voice was crisp. "I say I'll pay two hundred a week and expenses to a man who can follow specific directives and who can procure the people to carry them out."

"That's a good week's pay. Anything illegal?"

"There shouldn't be. Ed was inclined to trim his sails a little too closely in that respect. When you have a mind as devious as mine, illegality becomes an unnecessary luxury."

He considered the clear blue eyes in the candid face. "I haven't heard anything yet I can hang a nail on, Mrs. Sanders."

"I'm sure you're giving me credit for a little common sense. Before I reach the point of no return with you I want a reaction. I think you understand me. You asked if it was illegal, and I said no. If you asked if it was ethical, I might feel it necessary to tell you that a clear two hundred a week buys up a few ethics. My late husband had ethics. I prefer a bank account."

This woman left no snagged threads at all; Johnny made one more try. "How about a for instance on a directive, Mrs. Sanders?"

For an instant he thought she was going to refuse, and then she changed her mind. "All right. Follow me closely, now; this is a little complicated. Some time ago a jeweler came to me—in my business I get referrals all the time—with a story of having been tricked by his partner. I checked and found out his story was true. I always do check, because over the years I've found that countermeasures such as we specialize in rarely result in an official protest if there has been an original wrong. Too much dirty linen would be exposed."

She knuckled a hand and scrubbed it briskly in the other palm. "I thought about it for a week. Then I had Ed Russo contact Tim Connor and three unemployed actors, one of them a woman. I set up a timetable for them, and for once they followed it perfectly. On a day like today, for example, the woman was sent to the jeweler where the wrong was to be righted, and she purchased an expensive watch of a type uncommon enough that the jeweler could not in reason have very many in stock. This watch was taken to a man who does work for us, and the expensive moment was removed and a very cheap movement substituted. The tampered watch was then returned to the woman. Three or four days later, in the early morning a man of the group went in to this same jeweler and bought an identical watch. This, too, was taken to our man, the expensive movement removed and the cheap movement substituted. An hour after the first man left the store, the second man went in and bought up *all* the watches of that style which were left in the store. Because of the price and style of the item there shouldn't be too many; regardless, it is his job to see that he gets them all, from counters, vault and windows. Hard on the heels of his departure the first man came back and returned the watch he had bought earlier the same morning, only now of course it contained the substituted cheap movement. On a returned item the store's watchmaker will automatically check the merchandise as a matter of course, but where is the watchmaker who will take the back off the case and check the watch movement inside?"

Helen Sanders smiled as Johnny leaned forward in his chair, trying to follow her story. "In the meantime, Tim Connor had contacted a man he knew on the District Attorney's Racket Squad. Tim told this man that he'd bought an expensive watch for his girl, had had trouble with it, had taken it to another jeweler, and that the second jeweler had told him that it had a cheap, inferior movement in it and that he'd been rooked. The Racket Squad man naturally said let's go and see this crooked jeweler. Tim led his little party on the scene and accused the clerk of selling his girl a doctored watch. The clerk denied it, naturally, and called out the watchmaker, who took the back off the case of the woman's watch and was confounded by what he found. The Racket Squad man moved in and demanded to see all other watches of that type in stock. They could only have one; the returned one which also had a cheap, inferior movement. Try explaining it to a Racket Squad man some time."

Johnny blew out his breath. "Lady, when you said you had a devious mind it was the understatement of all time." He thought back over it, step by step. "Foolproof. A perfect frame."

Helen Sanders nodded. "All purchases are for cash, strictly. Phony names, except for the woman complainant, and phony addresses. It's an expensive operation, but the man who wanted the job done paid fifteen hundred dollars for it.

142

Paid it cheerfully. He didn't know how it was done; he didn't care. He saw the result." She looked at Johnny across the desk. "Well?"

"Let me sleep on it. I'll call you."

"An amendment. I'll call you." Helen Sanders rose and stubbed out her cigarette vigorously; there was an air of quiet competence in everything this woman did, Johnny reflected. She smiled at him again, the sudden, bright smile which made her appear so much younger. "I think we'll get along, Johnny." She sobered then, considering him. "There is one change I'm going to make in the operation. Ed Russo used to come to this office for his instructions. I find that a needless involvement. You will in the future receive your instructions from a third party who will be connected with both offices, but will appear in neither."

"You mean you're installin' an overseer? I might not like that."

"You won't have any trouble with the overseer."

"I could feel different about it."

"You won't. When you learn who it is."

He considered her carefully. "The overseer know about this? How's he gonna feel about it?"

Helen Sanders' smile was crisp. "I'll have to admit he warned me not to approach you. He felt you were—shall we say—unstable? On the other hand, I need a man with your seeming flair for direct action. The decision I reserved for myself, of course." She moved out from behind her desk. "We've talked enough, until you give me your answer. I think we're all practical people. I risked only one thing, actually, in approaching you. An outright 'no' might have made it necessary to transfer the operation to another hotel. A hotel is a perfect cover for all-hours and all kinds of comings and goings. It would have been inconvenient, but it was worth the risk to get the right man."

Lady, you just think you only risked one thing, Johnny thought. He felt a rising excitement gnawing at him as he stood up to confront Helen Sanders. He had to get out of there . . . he needed time to think—

"I'll call you in the morning," Helen Sanders was saying firmly as she walked with him to the door. Absently he noted that she had a nice way of moving; she must be forty, forty-five, but she was sure giving it a battle.

He reached the street without being fully conscious if he

had used the elevator or the stairs. He looked for a drug-store and a phone booth, and then changed his mind. He started to look for a cab and changed his mind again. He set out for the hotel at a steady pace, his mind churning.

He nearly walked past the foyer entrance as he plowed along; he turned in and went directly up to his room. Sassy jumped up from a kittenish sprawl to greet him; he ruffled her fur absently for a moment, kicked off his shoes and stretched out on the bed. He stared up at the ceiling for a long time.

He roused himself finally, stretched and walked over to the window. He was surprised to find it dark outside. He drew the shade to three-quarter length and returned to the bed. With hands locked behind his head he resumed his critical inspection of the ceiling.

When he stirred finally his left arm had fallen asleep; he rubbed the circulation back into it and picked up his phone. "Ring eight-fifteen, Edna," he told the operator when she came on the line. He listened to the insistent *brrrrtt*.

"Mike? Johnny. You got time to run down to my room a minute? Looks like you're gonna be my new boss, so I ought to start gettin' in right."

"You mean she—"

"After what you told her she did it anyway. A whim of iron, that lady. Come on down and let's talk it over." He replaced the phone gently, looked around the room, rose from the bed and extinguished the room light. Back at the bed he sat down on its edge, letting his eyes gradually accustom themselves to the room's darkness. He felt a sharp sting in his ankle; Sassy was diligently exercising her claws on it. Johnny reached down, picked her up and put her in his lap; even in the darkness he could make out the white puffball of the kitten's figure as she settled down contentedly.

Johnny sat and listened to the quiet in the room, his eyes on the thin pencil of light under the edge of his door. Beside him the phone rang, and he jumped; in his preoccupation it was a jarring, unexpected sound. He picked it up hurriedly. "Yeah?"

"This is Edna, Johnny. There's a lady here to see you. A Mrs. Barnes."

"Tell her—tell her I'll be down in a few minutes, Edna."

He waited impatiently in the short pause before Edna's voice came back on the line. "I don't see her in the lobby.

She came on the house phone before when you were talking, and I couldn't connect you. Could she have gone upstairs? I didn't—"

"Listen, Edna," Johnny said rapidly. "Find her, or have someone find her for you. Hold her in the lobby. I'll be down shortly." He hung up quickly and waited for the telephone noise to die out in his ear so that he could again concentrate on room sound. His eyes again picked up the line of light under the door, and he settled back on the bed. He stiffened as his ear picked up a faint, alien sound, and his unwinking stare focused on the line of light as he waited for it to widen in indication that the door had been silently opened.

The line remained constant, however, and the noise repeated itself, direction indistinguishable in the darkness. Johnny wrenched his eyes away from the light at the door and stared blindly around the room. He became conscious suddenly of the kitten on his lap; the small head was turned at right angles toward the window. Johnny tensed; he could picture the pink nose wrinkling as Sassy tested the air —had she felt a current of air from the window being raised slowly and almost quietly from the outside?

He bounded from the bed, carrying the kitten with him; he flattened himself against the end wall, out of line with window and bed. Over his shoulder he strained his eyes back to the door, but the thin line of light remained stationary, and then in the middle of his breath of relief the night around him erupted in gunfire.

He couldn't count the sharp explosions; in the small space the noise was deafening. Blue flame pierced the window shade, which jumped crazily in the blur of shots. Johnny found himself on his knees as he listened to the slugs tearing up his mattress, and then his ears tingled with the quiet. On his belly he snaked across the floor; he reached up and grabbed the bottom edge of the smoldering shade and yanked it completely off the window. He tightened against another fusillade, but there was silence. He could smell the shade burning at the edges of the bullet holes, and he ground out the creeping edges of fire with his palms.

He rose cautiously and angled a look out at the fire escape. There was no movement in the night; he leaned forward by slow degrees, and verified that the fire escape was empty. A flutter caught his eye; he strained to make out the

145

object—paper?—which stirred lightly in the after-sundown breeze as it appeared to be caught on the iron handrail.

His eyes swam from the intensity of his stare, but he could see no details on the flapping material. In stockinged feet he went lightly to the closet and fumbled out two coat hangers. Back at the partially raised window he listened to the silence in the outside world. It was not silent in the hotel; already he could hear noises in the corridor. He had to move and move quickly.

He set himself, and in one quick lunge reached out the few feet with the extended coat hangers, trapped the light-weight material on the handrail between them, and pulled it back into the room. His fingers told him it was cloth; in the darkness he could make out no details, and he wanted no light in that room. Hurriedly he put on his shoes, shoving the cloth in his pocket. He opened his room door carefully and eased out into the corridor. Once out he ran for the fire door, paying no attention to the curious heads in the open doorways.

On the first landing he stopped and pulled the piece of cloth from his pocket; he looked down for an instant at a patch-pocket, apparently torn from a black-and-white checked jacket, and jammed it back in his pocket. He raced down five flights of stairs, caroming off walls on the sharp turns. He burst down off the mezzanine through the lobby, and in the foyer he saw them, between the inner and outer glass doors.

Mike Larsen whirled as Johnny rushed in, his lips a dark gash in his white face. His staring eyes were locked blindly upon Johnny's face; at his elbow Lorraine Barnes' hypnotized glare was fixed rigidly on the ugly, black automatic in Mike Larsen's right hand.

CHAPTER 15

Glad you got the gun away from her, Mike," Johnny said casually to the little tableau.

Mike Larsen's voice was harsh. "We've gone a little bit beyond that foolishness, Johnny. A little bit beyond." He looked at Lorraine Barnes, and Johnny looked, too. For the first time since he had known her the iron facade was cracked; her eyes were enormous. She swallowed, hard, and her voice was breathless.

"He said . . . Mike said—"

She swallowed again, and Johnny anticipated her. "That he'd killed me? His intentions were fine." He looked carefully at Mike Larsen, who moved back two paces, the negligently held gun equidistant between Johnny and Lorraine. Johnny wondered how long they could stand there a dozen feet from the street without interruption.

Mike must have wondered, too. He glanced out to the sidewalk; he's made up his mind, Johnny thought suddenly. He's over most of the shock; he's going to play the hand out. Mike's voice confirmed this in the next breath; he spoke almost normally. "Outside. My car's across the street. Be careful. Both of you."

Like an automaton Lorraine Barnes pushed through the outer glass doors. With the unwinking eye of the gun upon him Johnny followed and, on the sidewalk, breathed in the summer night's dry heat.

"Over there," Mike Larsen said quickly. He stood with his right hand thrust under his left armpit. "Second in line."

Second in line was not the MG; Johnny half turned in inquiry before his eyes caught the dull silvered spot on the dark sedan second in line where once there had been a door handle. He followed the sleepwalking Lorraine to the sedan, now just one more of a number of things all pointing in the same direction.

Mike tossed the car keys to Lorraine; he looked up and down the thinly peopled street. He watched Lorraine, but never so closely that a good measure of his attention wandered from Johnny. "Open it up and get under the wheel." He waited for her to comply; his voice was tight, and there was a sheen on his forehead as he addressed Johnny. "You now. Delicately." He smiled, almost pleasantly. "In my mind you're already dead, you know."

Johnny inched in the front seat beside Lorraine, doubling up his left leg and sitting on it. He could feel the car springs settle as the rear door slammed, and Mike's voice came again strongly, the relief in it evident. "Down to Ninth, Lorraine, and turn left."

Johnny turned his head carefully until he could see the back seat and Mike sitting with the gun in his lap. Mike looked almost jovial; he was pleased with himself. "That was my first really poor move, Johnny, upstairs just now. I panicked when you called me, because I realized that you knew. I'm glad it misfired; this gives me a chance to do the thing right."

"You're runnin' out of chances, boy," Johnny said softly. "Fast." He stared at the man in the back seat. "How could I have missed it?"

"Because I was able to throw just enough sand in your eyes as we went along," Mike replied comfortably. "I told you just enough about Connor to keep you from going to someone else." He paused as Lorraine Barnes made the left turn onto Ninth Avenue. "Left on Forty-fourth right here." He returned his attention to Johnny. "And I told you that Lorraine was having an affair with Sanders to forestall the possibility of your wondering if she was having an affair with me." He leaned forward slightly. "Down to Second Avenue, Lorraine, then right to the tunnel."

"Tunnel?" Johnny caught himself. When Mike had directed them east on Forty-fourth Johnny had assumed their destination to be the warehouse alley where Ed Russo had died in the rain. The tunnel . . . He looked at Mike. "We goin' out to the boat?"

"We are indeed. I realized belatedly that I can't stand the discovery of two more bullet-riddled bodies on the perimeter of our tight little circle. No . . . a boating accident is indicated."

Johnny's voice was husky. "There'll be an accident all right, Mike, but it's gonna happen to you. I'll leave you out there for good." His voice rose; he half surged up in the seat in the violence of the emotion that gripped him. "I'll leave parts of you all over Long Island Sound—" He broke off as the gun in Mike's lap rose up and considered him carefully.

"I wouldn't," Mike said quietly. "I have remarkably little to lose." He smiled thinly. "We'll have to put up with each other, until the boat ride."

Johnny seethed internally. He thought of the battered pier where the boat was moored, deserted even in the daytime.

148

Somewhere out there on the dark water he was going to find a way to turn the tables, and when he did it was going to be the end of the line for Mike Larsen.

"I was sorry about Ellen, you know," Mike said conversationally.

"Sorry!" Johnny said gutturally.

"Sanders was just an obstacle in my way," Mike continued, unperturbed. "Bobby Perry was a vicious little blackmailer who possessed a little dangerous knowledge. Ed Russo was getting close to adding two and two together, since he had knowledge that you didn't. I regretted none of them." His voice rose sharply. "Nonentities, sluts, bullet-bait!" With a visible effort he brought his voice back under control. He sounded properly regretful. "Ellen, though, was the factor which jiggered my little equation all out of shape."

The sedan veered left; Johnny looked around to see the yawning, white-mouthed tunnel entrance, and the multiplicity of signs—*Queens Midtown Tunnel*. Behind him Mike's voice resumed as they rolled through the winding ivory tube. "I'll never know why Ellen left the car that night. I had driven her over there myself; she was to have been my alibi for Sanders. I had previously arranged for her to deliver a kitten to Russo, and I was her transportation. A day or two later the fact of our having been in the neighborhood at the time of Sanders' death might have drawn a comment from Ellen; hardly anything more. I left her in the car for no more than five minutes; I knew I could count on Sanders, who was a methodical man. But Ellen left the car. I've wondered——"

He stopped talking as the car emerged from the whiteness of the tunnel into the night again; ahead of them the lights of the toll station loomed up. "I'd advise a little caution on the part of both of you here," Mike said in an altered voice as they eased to a stop. The wooden-faced Lorraine handed a quarter to the toll collector, and in seconds they were in motion again.

Johnny looked at the car lights ahead on the parkway, then back to the driver, who sat stiffly with eyes straight ahead on the road. What was on this woman's mind? "Watch out for the parkway turn-off," he advised her. "It's a little tricky at night."

Mike's laugh was pure amusement. "Johnny, our chauffeur is more familiar with the parkway turn-off than you are—and especially at night."

149

"You fluffed her off," Johnny said thoughtfully. "Lorraine was followin' you that night?"

"And just about every night since," Mike said harshly. He waited for his voice to level; he tried to restore it to its former tone of amused condescension. "It put me to a bit of trouble shaking her. Deliver me from women who love not wisely but too well. Her original intention, of course, was to find out my other interest."

"And your other interest was Helen Sanders," Johnny said. "You found out you could make a little time with her?"

"I found out I could marry her." The man in the back seat leaned forward suddenly. "Not a bad prospect for an odd-jobs man. I decided to let nothing stand in the way of the project."

"But she said she'd already decided to get a divorce—"

The laugh from the back seat was not amused this time. "A divorce takes time; too much time. For Helen Sanders, my type is not uncommon; I felt I had to shorten the gap. I had been thinking rather casually along these lines when I was suddenly given cause to accelerate my thinking. Even from a business standpoint Robert Sanders had never approved of me. He had accused me in the past of pandering to his wife's money-making greed by aiding and abetting her little schemes with which you're now familiar. He had taken the trouble to discover a situation in which I was vulnerable, legally perhaps. He threatened me with it. At the least it meant the end of my business usefulness to Helen Sanders, and, knowing that lady, I was afraid that it would be a case of out of sight, out of mind. I decided that I had a position to protect. I protected it and had the shock of a not uneventful life when I came out of that apartment areaway and found Ellen on the walk in close conversation with our little dove here. I didn't know in feet and inches how close they'd been, but obviously too close."

The car slowed; Johnny looked around in the lights and saw the black-lettered white sign, *Grand Central Parkway*. Lorraine inched around the sharp right-hand turn and crept out on the three-lane one-way highway. Johnny noticed these things automatically; his mind was still on the man in the back seat. "So you followed Ellen?"

"Of course. The situation was critical. She might tell anyone at all what she'd seen. Or imagined or surmised—all equally dangerous, so far as I was concerned. Our chaffeur's personal fortunes were involved; she was, I felt, a different breed of cat. I followed Ellen, lost her on the sidewalk due to your dramatics, left the car, came back and went upstairs."

"How in the hell did you find her?" Johnny demanded roughly.

"Simplicity itself. I felt sure you wouldn't register her, but in that case you'd have to tell Vic to prevent the possibility of his assigning a legitimate guest to the same room. When you were out of the way on your nightly round I went down to the desk and told Vic I was delivering something for you, and where had you put Ellen? Naturally, he told me. The one thing I didn't realize at the time was your previous personal connection with Ellen, and the rather primitive reaction you experienced surprised me. Alarmed me a little, to be truthful, to the extent of improvising a couple of smoke screens."

The sedan purred through the darkness. Johnny watched the lights of the oncoming cars on the other side of the divided highway as they appeared far down the road, to gradually brighten, loom up menacingly and hurtle on by. When he spoke his voice was tired. "How I could have been so blind . . . you and your fake skin pigmentation deficiency out on the boat, so you wouldn't have to take your shirt off. You couldn't take it off. You had the devil's own luck; Vic knew about you, but thinking that Lorraine was involved he shut down completely rather than say anything that might get her in more trouble."

"For different reasons," Mike said complacently, "I felt I had little to fear from either Vic or Lorraine. Oh, the lady here accused me, but I of course denied it, and entangled as she was herself she wasn't quite sure enough about me to make a move herself. She did take to following me, which was inconvenient."

Johnny sat with hands tightly clenched by his side as the sound of Mike Larsen's voice died away in the back seat; where had he gone wrong? He should have known, but how? Mike was right in one respect; the key pieces in the puzzle, the vital little bits of information had fallen into place too late.

He leaned forward and began to watch the turn-off signs as the realization came to him that they had been on the parkway for some time. He was in a hurry to get to the boat. "Glen Cove Road is the one we want."

"I know." Lorraine Barnes spoke for the first time since they had left the foyer of the hotel. Johnny looked curiously at her stiff features, and the white-knuckled hands on the wheel.

The sedan slowed under her guidance and eased gently down a curving exit road which bore off to the right; on the highway below she turned back left under the overpass. A roadside directional sign picked up in the headlights as they completed the turn listed the towns in the area with little black arrows pointing—Sea Cliff, Glen Cove, Roslyn, Locust Valley, Lattenburg, Bayville. They rode along the Glen Cove Road, and Johnny could see Lorraine watching for the Sea Cliff turn-off. Mike was right; it was not the first time she had driven this route.

Salt tang was fresh in the warm air as the car swung sharply left and then right again in a hundred yards and set off on the long diagonal paralleling the water, which could almost be felt. It was not quite ten, but most of the lights in the quiet houses of Sea Cliff were already out. In Glen Cove the lights were on in one restaurant; the first stop light was on the blinking yellow, the second still on the red and green. They by-passed the right angle swing through the center in favor of the little yellow signs proclaiming *Direct Route to Bayville.*

Johnny stretched cautiously in his cramped position in the front seat; his voice was soft. "Used to know every inch of this country when I was a raggedy-tailed kid." He looked directly at Lorraine behind the wheel. "You ever been down on the island below Bayville? Centre Island, they call it. Something to see. Estates, mansions, stone walls, high wooden fences. Palaces, they looked like to a kid. I've cut grass on half of 'em, there and over at Oyster Bay. There's at least one boat, cruiser size, goes with each house, and some of the Centre Islanders had channels cut in the rock so they could tie their boats up right under their front porches."

She took her eyes from the road in one quick flash to look at him sharply, then returned to her driving. The car's pace again slowed; Johnny could see her looking for the unmarked gravel road. At the sudden gap in the trees she braked and turned hard left, and they bumped down off the macadam as the tires crunched in the loose gravel. She tapped the brights and steered down the light-colored ribbon of road between the scrub trees and the tangled undergrowth. They ran out of the tree line, and tall, waving grass loomed up on either side of the sedan, and then the grass grew shorter and less dense and the dark pilings of the dock appeared in the headlights. Lorraine turned the car off onto the weeds and shut off the motor, and for an instant the only sound was the night breeze in the saw grass.

Johnny turned back to Mike Larsen as something occurred to him. "You sent the note in to Vic?"

Mike nodded; he was looking out at the pier. "Yes. Not one of my more inspired moments. Can't even think now why it seemed important at the time, except that things were popping a little too rapidly for my liking." He seemed to rouse himself as he looked back at Johnny. "I sent the trio who waylaid you outside of Lorraine's, too. Another little backfire that fizzled. I wanted you to blame Russo for it; he'd already become a headache to me. I thought you'd dismantle him on sight."

"The first fifteen seconds that I saw him afterward he tried to bet me fifty he could take me even. After sendin' out a losin' goon squad, it just didn't figure."

He had lost Mike's attention; from the back seat the automatic motioned at Lorraine. "You get out first." She complied, and Mike eased out on Johnny's side of the car, gun leveled. "You, Johnny."

Johnny got out a little stiffly; he stood erect and stretched leisurely. He looked up at the sky; the earlier haze had disappeared, and the night was clear. He fixed the stars in his mind; he knew now what he had to do, but he didn't know how much time he had in which to do it. Mike Larsen did not intend that three of them should return from this boat ride. Or even two of them, whether Lorraine Barnes realized it or not.

The beam of a flashlight came on in Mike's hand; he moved in a semicircle around Johnny and handed it to Lorraine. "You lead."

The loose fill grated under their feet, and the weeds whispered damply. Their footsteps echoed hollowly on the pier's timbers until they stood dockside to *Ye Olde Beaste.* Beneath their feet there was the faint hiss of water and the occasional slap of a slightly larger wave against a piling.

153

Against the night light of sky and stars the stubby masts of the moored boats danced in shadowy disorder.

"You first, Johnny, into the boat," Mike decided. "Drop down and take off the tarp. You keep the light on him, Lorraine, and if I see you going for a spanner, Johnny, that's it, right there." The white of his teeth showed in the blur of his features. "You could probably dive under the pier and get away; I know you're a fish in the water, but I think you'd rather get your hands on me."

How right you are, Mike Larsen, Johnny thought to himself as he swung down the piling ladder and reached for the deck with his feet. And I know how I'm going to do it. In the beam of light directed down at him from the pier above he knelt and loosened the ties on the tarp, bundled it and tossed it amidships.

"Take off the engine cowling." Mike's voice sounded right at his elbow; sound carried in the night. Johnny slid off the metal casing and stood it up in the stern. "Lorraine's coming down now. I'm watching you."

Johnny watched her cautious descent of the ladder; was it more typically feminine to be afraid of falling from the ladder between the creaking, barnacled pilings and the dark water line than of the gun in Mike Larsen's hand? He stepped up from the cockpit to the deck, scooping up an air-filled seat cushion as he did so. He reached up and lifted her down from the ladder, and with her body as a shield pushed the cushion under her arm, his whisper a breath in her ear. "Hang onto this." He released her; she made no sound, but her arm gripped the seat cushion.

Mike's carefully contrived face-forward descent, flashlight under an armpit and the gun in his free hand, was a strain on him. Explosive relief was again evident in his tone as he dropped the final three feet to the deck planking. "Now!"

Johnny smiled tightly to himself. He thinks he's crossed his last river. He doesn't know his white water is still ahead of him.

Mike pointed with the gun to the opposite side of the cockpit from his own station at wheel and throttle. "You, Johnny. Over there. Carefully." He groped in a locker cupboard behind him and tossed a fish knife to Lorraine. "When I say so cut the lines."

The cockpit sprang to trembling life as the engine roared, and Mike gunned it a time or two to make sure it had fully

154

caught. A flip of a switch and the port and starboard red and green lights came on, and the masthead running light.

"Cut the lines!" Mike had to raise his voice over the engine sound; he waited as Lorraine cautiously picked her way from stern to bow. Mike eased back delicately on the bar throttle as they inched away from the pier. In a boat as over-engined as *Ye Olde Beaste* slow speed was nearly as ticklish as high; long ago Mike had wound a strip of tape, now dirty and discolored, around the throttle bar at the point beyond which it was not safe to advance the lever arm.

Around them Long Island Sound glimmered black and slick as Lorraine came back and sat down to Johnny's left. They moved out beyond the point, and as the shoreline disappeared behind them a faint swell manifested itself even in the flat calm. An occasional wave slapped lightly under the bow and hissed along the water line; Mike touched the throttle bar and the engine took on a deeper note. The stern-heavy *Ye Olde Beaste* settled even more deeply in the water as the powerful propeller took hold, and the bow rose correspondingly steeper in pitch.

Johnny looked at the silvery wisps of spray filtering in over the stern, then up at the stars. With the toe of his right shoe he forced his left shoe off and in an unhurried movement picked it up in his toes and lifted it to where he could reach it with his hand without bending down. He placed it gently on the thwart beside him; he had a feeling it would not be long now. The gun should be no problem; Mike wanted no bullet holes. When Mike went for a spanner, or next attempted to position Johnny differently, possibly . . .

Mike Larsen moved out a step from his helmsman post, his left hand negligently on the wheel behind him. The gun which had dangled at his side in his boat-handling preoccupation swung up and around in deliberate presentation. Mike's voice was crisp; his face was calm. "Sit still, Lorraine. Johnny—" His left hand left the wheel and groped in the locker beside him, and in the second his eyes veered fractionally Johnny stood up, picked up his shoe and threw it at the throttle bar.

At the short range of the crowded cockpit he scored a direct hit on the lever arm, and Mike Larsen yelled hoarsely as the arm jumped the restraining tape and jammed at the full-speed end of the bar. Johnny crouched as the engine boomed in a long unused explosion of power, and *Ye Olde*

155

Beaste jumped forward beneath them. The engine sound was fantastic; the stern flattened, and the bow canted higher. The boat began to shudder uncontrollably, and Mike Larsen by main strength clawed himself off the cockpit rim against which he had been flung and stared wild-eyed at the water shipping in over the stern. Beneath their feet a deep grinding noise punctuated splintering sounds as the hull began to disintegrate under the pounding of the water, and a high-pitched whine filled the air.

The white-faced man dived for the throttle as black water spurted through the sprung seams; his frantic grab jerked the lever arm from full speed to zero, and Johnny leaned forward, picked up Lorraine Barnes and threw her over the side. Behind him the stern rose like a cork; the high-canted bow dipped deeply and plunged its blunt nose into an oncoming swell like a fat man stabbing his toe into the ground in the middle of a hundred-yard dash. There was a shivering crash; Mike Larsen screamed shrilly as the heavy stern rose inexorably in a monstrously grotesque cartwheel while disintegrated planking flew like popcorn.

Johnny went over the side in the deepest dive he could manage as the boat stood on its nose; he hit the Sound's unyielding bottom with an impact that nearly stunned him. His ears rang both with the concussion of his own dive and the nearby cataclysmic dull thunderclap of sound as *Ye Olde Beaste* pounded back into the water, upside down. He struggled back up in a frenzy of arms and legs, surfaced and roughly sleeved the water from his eyes. The night was filled with a hissing, bubbling noise, and seventy yards ahead a black blot that bore no resemblance to a boat disappeared altogether in a leisurely curving arc.

Johnny swam to the spot in a thrashing scramble. He criss-crossed back and forth through the gaseous bubbles and the little pieces of flotsam that popped to the surface all around him. No man could possibly survive such an impact, but still he swam. The bubbles weakened and died, and the flotsam drifted away; the only sound in Johnny's ears was the water awash on his shoulders as he plowed stubbornly on his course, until he was sure.

No man had survived.

He turned and swam in the opposite direction. He bored into the chop, breasted it and trod water while he scanned the surface of the Sound. A faint sound to his right sent him

156

strongly in that direction, riding high in the water. He saw her, finally; Lorraine Barnes rose and fell in the inky swell, her upper body across the air-filled cushion to which she clung like grim death. She sobbed when she saw him; her hair was like wet seaweed all over her face, and her nose was bleeding from the force with which she had struck the water.

"M-Mike!" she choked, and Johnny reared up alongside her, unbelieving.

"I ought to leave you out here, you fool!"

She didn't even hear him. "Mike, Mike, oh, Mike!"

The thick surge of anger swelled in his throat and then died. This was Vic's wife. Mike had tried to frame her twice and would certainly have killed her tonight, and still she could call for him. This was Vic's wife, about as wrong as a woman could be, but he had to get her back to shore. "Shut up and listen to what I tell you."

A stinging little wavelet slapped her in the face, and she spat a mouthful of chop. "We'll d-drown!" She strangled. "Drown!"

"Not in this pond." Johnny reached down and pulled off his other shoe. "I could swim it both ways, if I had to." He pulled the belt out of his slacks and peeled them off. He ripped and tore at shirt and T-shirt until he felt a blessed freedom. He looked up at the stars, orienting himself, and then turned back to the sobbing woman. He pulled her clothes off in great, bunched handfuls.

He bounced erect in the water for another look at the stars, then settled back. "Put your left hand on my right shoulder," he told her curtly. "Hold the cushion in your right armpit. Don't fight it; let it balance you. And hang onto me."

He set out at a steady beat and in three hundred yards had made the adjustment for the drag on his right side. He bored persistently through the rising swells, with head turned to one side to breathe deeply between onslaughts. Twice he paused to check the stars again and altered course slightly; the only noise he heard beside the roar of water in his ears was an occasional animal-like sound from his companion.

He swam strongly, thinking not at all of time or distance, and was surprised when the dark mass of the shoreline blotted out his waterlogged horizon. He had thought they were farther out; he shook his head to clear his ears of the benumbing water pressure and tried to listen. If the noise

157

he heard was surf, and not just the roaring of his own ears, then he had missed the target. Surf meant rocks, and rocks meant trouble. He turned and swam parallel to the thickening blur of the shoreline, and between two waves he lifted his head and saw the little forest of masts. Again he laboriously shifted course and doggedly carved out his watery path until a blacker shadow in the variegated darkness transformed itself into the lee side of a cabin cruiser. He worked his way around to the stern and transferred the nearly limp Lorraine back to her cushion. He pulled himself up to cockpit level on the boat, then set his teeth and brutally muscled his heavy body over and in. The dead-weight lift after all the time in the water was nearly more than he could manage; from the chest down he felt as though he weighed a ton.

He waited for his chest to stop heaving and looked down for the woman bobbing below him. "Watch yourself coming aboard; I'm too pooped to lift you clean." He didn't know if she had heard him; he braced himself, reached far over, grabbed her under the armpits and lifted until the blood hammered in his ears. She scraped her thighs coming over the side and moaned as she tumbled in a white lump in the bottom of the boat.

Johnny stood up when he could breathe again; he didn't know why he still felt driven, but he couldn't take the rest that common sense urged upon him. He twisted the hasp from a locker and rummaged inside. He threw handfuls of clothing at the white body and found a pair of paint-stained trousers for himself. He could hear her crying as he straightened up wearily, the deep sobs of exhaustion. For an instant he didn't relaize she was trying to say something. "—make it up to V-Vic . . . I w-will—I will!"

He spat salt spume and another taste and walked up to the bow. He jumped heavily to the deck of the next moored boat and again to the one beyond. When he reached a piling ladder he slogged his way up it, the rough timbers reminding his stockinged feet that he should have scouted the ransacked locker for shoes. He was too tired to go back.

He hauled himself erect on the splintered pier topside and automatically turned to look once more out over the Sound. Unconsciously his hands hooked into claws. How could you do it, Mike? We were friends, you and I. And Vic. I hope Vic never knows that you've left him with very nearly as little as you left me.

158

He started the long trek out to the road; the car keys were at the bottom of Long Island Sound, and they needed transportation. And the police had to be notified. The police . . . he grimaced wryly. He stumbled off the dock timbers onto the gravel, and his heels bit stingingly as his weaving walk jarred him from side to side. His ears still sang from the water-wash, and his bare arms and shoulders were encrusted with a film of sticky salt. He tried to concentrate on steering a straight course on the lighter colored gravel road which led up to the highway and renounced it in favor of putting one foot before the other. The swash in his ears died out gradually, and he could hear the high-pitched whisper of the night breeze in the scrub pines, mournfully persistent.

He put down his head and walked on.